Hear Us Fade

Also by David Hogan

The Last Island

Hear Us Fade

DAVID HOGAN

BETIMES BOOKS

First published in the English language in Dublin, Ireland, in 2021
by Betimes Books CLG

www.betimesbooks.com

ISBN 978-1-9161565-7-9

Cover image © Sergey Nehaev

Cover design by JT Lindroos

For Buzz

TABLE OF CONTENTS

Part I

10:37 AM – 1:01 PM
June 16, 2029

1

Rex Nightly never considered how painful it is to torture a man.

His thighs burn; his arms ache; his temples throb. His gums are numb, and his heart is palpitating. He has peculiar, cherry-sized bumps on his forearms. Maybe it's just a reaction to the CELEBRATATE[1] he took an hour earlier to relieve the spasms in his lower back. Or not. Either way, he's finding precious little to *celebratate* at the moment.

The honorable and hefty Abbot Swenson, Governor of the State of California – and the man that Rex and his friend, Urban McChen, are currently torturing – doesn't appear too worse off for the experience. Lying semi-conscious in the claw-foot bathtub, the blindfolded governor has small lagoons of sweat under his arms and his forehead is as furrowed as thick corduroy, but that seems to be the extent of it. For all of Rex's and Urban's wearying labors of abducting, tying-up, gagging, prodding, and zapping, they don't seem to be getting anywhere. Rex's lower back is starting to feel better, true, but that's a small consolation.

---

1 Side effects of CELEBRATATE include the loss of hearing, smell, vision, taste, touch, and consciousness as well as instant death.

Urban hands the Taser to Rex and then raises his hands, palms out, in a gesture of surrender, as if he doesn't know how to proceed, as if the whole thing hadn't been his idea to begin with. Rex glares at Urban but isn't sure that his expression can be seen through the half-leg of pantyhose that covers his face. He glances at the mirror above the medicine cabinet and can't tell if it's fogged up from their exertions or it's the peanut-colored stocking filtering his vision.

"It's too much," he says. The governor hasn't moved for the last few minutes, and Rex is having difficulty sucking air through his nylon-compressed nose.

"Just a little more," Urban replies, raising the red ski mask from his mouth without disturbing the heavy ponytail hanging from the back of it. "Until he gives us what we want."

Rex sighs. The governor is becoming less and less responsive, but this only makes Urban more determined. This can't end well. Not that it started well. There are a number of reasons why Rex didn't want to be involved in the first place. Beginning with the idea itself.

Kidnap the governor?

Deposit him in Rex's bathtub?

Gently torture him?

Even if it's for a good cause, the purported greater good, these are extreme measures. As if Rex would have any idea about torturing someone. Rex, who's never started a fight in his life. Who recycles more than 97% of what he consumes. Who over-tips bad waiters out of pity. Who writes epic poetry, teaches high-school English, is 'well liked' in a majority of student surveys, and serves soup to the homeless on Tuesday nights.

He still isn't sure how Urban convinced him to bring the governor to his own penthouse. True, the governor was going to be in San Francisco at a meeting across the street, which made the intercept easy. And, true, they couldn't be seen leading a tied-up and blindfolded man through the streets of the city, so proximity to an available bathroom or similar hidden chamber was paramount. And yes, Rex has a key to the seldom-used service elevator in his building. But still.

The governor's head bobs twice. He moans and then either smiles or swallows or grimaces. Rex isn't sure. Urban puts the governor's eCatt to the man's mouth.

"You can make it stop anytime, governor," Urban says. "By stopping the execution. Easiest thing in the world. All you have to do is say 'stay.' Like talking to your dog."

The governor doesn't respond, not verbally anyway. His left arm rises and falls and his middle finger twitches, but that's all. He's either stubborn or incapacitated. And he'll have to buy a new suit after this incident is over, though the red power tie that's draped over his right shoulder might be salvageable.

Rex looks out the open bathroom door and through the penthouse to the terrace, twenty-three floors high in a San Francisco sky that's murky with smoke. The forest fires that have been uncontained for more than three months are approaching the coast. He briefly questions why every Californian isn't pitching in with a bucket, hose or shovel to save what's left of their state. Why isn't every personal drone dumping water or fire retardant on at-risk homes? Do they think the fires will eventually counteract the coastal flooding, or vice versa? Are they savoring the lethal irony? Though what his fellow Californians, their drones, and their ironic sensibilities are doing is concern for another time. Right now, his priority is the kidnapped governor, undependably positioned and possibly unconscious in his bathtub.

Rex snorts through his compressed nose as he hands the Taser back to Urban. There's a moldy smell somewhere, but he can't tell whether it's coming from the governor, the toilet, or the hosiery. Rex believes he might be allergic to nylon blends and briefly ponders the purpose of pantyhose. He can discover only two: to hide varicose veins and engage in criminal activity.

"You're making me do this, governor," Urban says and tasers him again, 125 volts injected into the man's muffin top.

The governor gulps and emits the same strange backward hiccup-like sound he made the first two times Urban zapped him. Within that time, Rex and Urban have entered into two separate and lengthy dialogues as to whether or not that hiccup-like utterance is, in fact, laughter, which Rex believes, or induced indigestion, which Urban believes. Either way, Rex doesn't want to discuss it for a third time and makes no comment as the uncertain noise echoes against the bathroom tiles.

The governor's legs begin to quiver, and Rex bends to hold them. As Rex's nose approaches the governor's body, he inhales the singular aroma that's created when flesh meets current. Rex doesn't want to hurt the governor. Not permanently. Or even temporarily. He doesn't want the governor to suffer any more than is necessary. Or at all. There's enough pain in the world.

He worries that the governor will lose control of his bladder or sphincter if they continue to electrify him. Rex makes a mental note that the next time – should he ever find himself in the unenviable position of torturing another person – he'll request that the victim empty both bladder and bowels before the proceedings. Or else wear adult diapers.

The governor's legs grow heavy as his pants ride up and expose the bloated tentacles of his cold, gray and heavy legs. Rex releases them and stands up.

The way Urban had described it, this whole undertaking would be uncomplicated and trouble-free: They'd kidnap the governor, provoke him into issuing a stay of execution, and then release him. One, two, three, and a man's life is saved. Easy peasy. No permanent damage done. Rex can't count the number of times Urban berated him about the evils of capital punishment, endlessly repeating that state-sanctioned murder is revengeful, cruel, and unjust, a malignant melanoma on the thin skin of American democracy.

Though Rex lacks the passionate intensity of Urban, that doesn't mean he wants his beloved California – which has long been ambiguous on the death penalty – sullied as the last place in the Western world to legally kill a man. He'd like to save California from that indignity. But more than that, he can't say. This isn't even his natural country. He'd endured a frozen, hockey-based childhood in Edmonton, Canada, where the death penalty had been abolished in 1967 and had never given the issue a second thought until he moved to the States and befriended Urban.

Rex has often wondered why, in 2029, Americans remain enamored with their ability to inflict violence, exalting in their pistols, rifles, personal armed drones, fighter jets, aircraft carriers, bio agents, neutrons, and nukes. Is it that their wars are fought elsewhere? They're a friendly and open people for the most part. He'd married one after all. Then again, every country feeds its appetite for violence in some way (*hockey?*) and maybe the American appetite is simply the most unapologetic. Also, he's inflicting a degree of violence right now, so who's he to judge.

Another reason why he agreed to help Urban is as trite as it is persuasive: friendship. Urban is a devoted friend. Rex has been betrayed by so-called friends at least three times in the past, once for a better dorm room in college (which he could forgive), once for a teaching job at an elite private high school (which he could also forgive), and once for a foul-mouthed, alcoholic Scottish woman that he was dating (which he couldn't forgive, even if he'd been looking for an excuse to break up with her at the time). Urban would never do any of those things. The man takes to friendship like a tumor to soft tissue, and the only way to end it is to excise him with a surgeon's pitilessness that Rex does not possess.

"We have to let him go," he says.

"If we do, a man dies," Urban responds. "We'll be the murderers."

"That man is being executed by the government. Not us."

"But if we can prevent a murder and don't do it ... that would make us accessories."

"I'd rather be a handbag than a torturer."

Urban glances at Rex through the eyeholes of his red ski mask but remains speechless. Now it's Rex who's making inappropriate jokes, and he feels infected. The governor rolls onto his left flank and snorts. A second later, Urban lets him have it again, a deft shock from the Taser just below the clavicle. The Governor backward hiccups into another gulp of laughter or indigestion, and Rex thinks that the governor might even be enjoying this somehow.

"I don't understand," Urban says and, more in frustration than anything else, shocks a colorless blotch on the governor's thick neck.

The governor laughs then respectively gags, backward hiccups, laughs, gags, chokes, backward hiccups and then laughs again until his head plops onto his chest. A tomblike silence fills the bathroom. Rex and Urban eye each other through their respective head covers, and then turn to the governor, gray and silent in the tub. Rex takes a deep and moldy breath through the pantyhose as Urban splashes water from the faucet onto the governor's face. Rex places his index and middle fingers firm against the carotid artery in the governor's wet neck.

"Either I'm the worst pulse taker in the world," he says. "Or his heart's stopped beating."

2

Billy 'The Goat' Wharton sits across from two armed guards in a driverless van.

He looks out the small window on the side of the van and sees a spiking, undulating carpet of fire, cardinal red and crow black on the distant mountains. Twigs, embers, and trash, aflame and aflight, glide toward the van but don't collide with it. They veer away in the final moments as if they too, like the inmates that Billy'd passed on his last walk, don't want to get too close. A tsunami of smoke and soot approaches from the distance, and Billy can imagine no better observance of his demise: California radiating and glowing like he'll soon be.

"From one fire to another," Billy says sociably, but neither of the guards responds. Billy'd been informed that they probably wouldn't talk to him during transit, but he's always been a companionable sort and believes he can win them over.

"If I get scared in the electric chair, will one of you hold my hand?" he tries, but again gets nothing back. These two are tough. He feels as bleak and lonely as the torched landscape as he realizes that to these two guards and to all his friends on death row – but not yet to himself – he's already dead.

For on this day, June 16, 2029, Billy Wharton is to be the last person executed in the United States of America. There are seven elderly justices on the Supreme Court who, by all accounts, are going to rule tomorrow, in *Penny-Miller v. Georgia*, that execution is a cruel and unusual punishment.

Or undependably administered.

Or ethnically, racially, and geographically biased.

Or the result of mistakes, misunderstandings, and misperceptions.

Or incompetent legal representation.

Or that the Bible's pithy 6th Commandment – 'Thou shall not kill' – should persuade any Judeo-Christian–based nation to refrain from doing so.

Whatever the reasons, someone will have to be the last man executed in the United States, and Governor Abbot Swenson and the State of California believe they have just the man in Billy Wharton. Billy'd confessed to killing eight people – though the police continue to maintain it was nine.

Despite the confession, Billy wasn't sure if he killed anybody at all. He'd suffered a blackout at the time of the murders, and his confession had been coerced by two wily and unscrupulous detectives feeding him details. They'd locked him in a room and berated him for 19 straight hours on a diet of saltines, cottage cheese and milk. Un-medicated, nauseous, and exhausted, Billy finally broke, but he refused to say that he killed the ninth person as a closing act of resistance. He wouldn't give them everything.

This exclusion caused problems for the prosecution at Billy's trial. "Why would a man confess to killing eight, but not nine, people?" Billy's lawyer asked repeatedly. "What difference does it make?"

The prosecution countered with speculation. Billy didn't confess to killing the ninth person because he was embarrassed. But he wasn't embarrassed that he *killed* the ninth person. No, Billy was fine with that. What embarrassed him was that he'd subsequently *eaten* the brain, liver, and big toes of the final person. Billy was a flesh-eater, that's what the prosecution claimed.

Billy didn't reliably know if he'd ingested that ninth person any more than if he'd killed the previous eight and, furthermore, didn't believe that embarrassment was a credible emotion for a serial killer. That didn't stop the media from labelling him 'The Goat,' even though Billy had been a strict vegetarian since his mid-teens, avoiding meat of any kind – with the possible late exception of human.

The trouble was that Billy had been off his meds at the time of the alleged murders and cannibalism. A few years before his arrest, he'd been seeing a psychiatrist for mood, sexual, personality, and OCD issues, and the shrink had prescribed a number of antipsychotic, anti-manic, antianxiety, and antidepressant drugs. At his trial, Billy revealed that the price of this combination of drugs had risen over 1,700% in the months before his alleged crimes, and he could no longer afford them. He'd ordered a reasonably priced and illegal shipment from Germany, but this had been late in arriving. *That* was why he'd stopped taking his meds.

Surprisingly to Billy and his lawyer, this revelation elicited sympathy from neither judge nor jury. (At his appeal, his new lawyer disclosed that Billy's psychiatrist had been taking payments from the manufacturers of these drugs, but this information was disregarded.)

The only drug that Billy had willingly stopped on his own – when he found that he could no longer reasonably control his arms, eyes, legs, or tongue – was the antipsychotic FLIPOZINE[2]. All too often when under the influence of the drug, he'd end up looking one way and sticking his tongue out the other or staggering down the sidewalk like a newborn giraffe. This had made eating, drinking, and hooking up with women extremely difficult. Because Billy never liked meeting women online. Despite his elephantine ears, he was 'sensibly handsome in real life,' as a former girlfriend had once said. He wanted women to see that right off. Before the FLIPOZINE, he'd done well with the ladies. But after starting the drug, if he were lucky enough to get a woman into his bed, the difficulties began. He often ended up tonguing her kneecaps or attempting to penetrate her armpit. So, yeah, he stopped that one, but you can't blame him.

Now he feels the heat as a giant wave of smoke and soot washes over the van. The interior grays, and it becomes harder to breathe. The armed guards across from him slowly become shadows, colorless sentries at their posts. But they remain upright as he bends over and puts his head between his knees to avoid inhaling the acidic air. He wonders if the software that drives the van has been programmed for such a situation. He'd gone to prison just as driverless cars were becoming legal and doesn't know how far they've come. He's heard stories of bugs and cyberattacks that had fifty cars piling up on the interstate or a half-dozen smashed into the same parking spot. But he'd heard lots of stories in prison.

---

2   Side effects of FLIPOZINE include uncontrollable movements of your lips, tongue, nose, eyes, ears, arms, legs, toes, and sphincter, as well as instant death.

One of the guards across from him starts coughing, and the other covers his face with his shirtsleeve. Billy slides from his seat, and the guards don't object or even seem to notice. His hands are cuffed behind him, and this causes him to land hard on his left shoulder on the floor. It hurts but doesn't seem to have dislocated. The air is clearer on the floor and gives him time to think before meeting God. He's never been too sure about any of that religious stuff, but he does know that now, on the road to his execution, is not the best time to debate His existence.

If anything, now is the time to think how he'd like to be remembered, for there's a good chance he will be remembered, if only on WikiKiller. What he'd like people to know is that, despite the alleged eight or nine carcasses littering his past, he's not a bad person. A person who made a mistake, perhaps even a big mistake, but far from evil. He'd like to be remembered as kind of like a suicide who jumped off a building and onto a person's head. It's tragic (for sure); it's manslaughter (possibly); but mostly it's a mistake. A suicide shouldn't be punished because any single mistake, no matter how awful the consequences – and even if committed eight or nine times – doesn't make a person evil. Not in a greater cosmic sense. And in the greater cosmos, what other sense is there?

Billy would like to ask the guards if they would kindly edit his page on WikiKiller in the coming months, but both of them are gagging and drooling. He'd like them and the interested public to know that it's critical to distinguish between active and passive acts. And that except for the alleged killings and eating, Billy's mistake had been of the passive variety. He tried to make this point at his sentencing, but the stiff-backed, injudicious Judge was having none of it. He said Billy showed a 'lack of remorse.' Billy objected (through his lawyer), but the Judge would not engage Billy (or his lawyer) in a discussion of what remorse was in a greater cosmic sense and, without a proper definition, how could the Judge possibly know if anyone lacked it?

Billy's lawyer also tried to make the case that Billy was a good man and an indispensable member of the community. Among other things, he'd saved six Pit Bulls and four Dobermans from rescue organizations and once remained in bed for 16 straight weeks for a NASA study. Nonetheless, with all that – with all that Billy had been and could be – the Judge sentenced him to death with all the consideration of a short order cook slapping another quarter-pounder on the grill.

Subsequently, Governor Abbot Swenson, looking for something bold and newsworthy to launch his presidential campaign with, hurried the appeals process and temporarily reinstituted the electric chair as a legal means of execution. ("Let's go out with a shocker," he'd said.) The governor wanted to make sure Billy got in under the electrified wire before the Supreme Court ruled on *Penny-Miller v. Georgia* so he could use Billy's death to launch his campaign for president. (In contrast, the respective governors of Texas, Georgia, Utah, and Tennessee immediately suspended all executions.) Now, because of an unscrupulous drug-maker, an unethical doctor, an indifferent judge, an unsympathetic jury, and an overambitious politician, Billy's name would be brought up in finger-wagging conversations as a murderer, cannibal, and the last man to be executed in the United States of America.

He hears a mix of spitting, choking, and wheezing from the guards. He can barely make out the tops of their heads through the smoke. One or both of them are gasping now. The coughing has stopped. So Billy does what he does best: He waits. He puts his nose to the cold, dirty floor of the van and waits.

One of the guards falls. The other reaches out his arm and calls something, a warning perhaps or a curse. Billy waits and inhales the dust and mold from the floor, resisting the urge to sneeze. A few moments later, the second guard falls, tipping like the final bowling pin, until he too strikes the floor. Billy feels the vibration on his cheek.

The van slows to a stop.

The engine shuts off.

The guards don't move.

Billy questions why he alone has retained consciousness. It might have something to do with the size of his ears, the abundance of cartilage maybe, or that they act as a sort of filter. But now even his ears are not enough; he feels woozy and weak. He can wait no longer, or he too will lose consciousness. He nudges one guard with his foot and gets no response.

Billy sidles next to the closest guard. He turns his back and scoots up so that his hands are near the guard's belt buckle. After several minutes of struggling, he manages to reach into the guard's pocket with one of his handcuffed hands. He finds nothing but an orange hard candy. It looks tasty and he can't remember the last time he had one, but he has no way to unwrap it and get it into his mouth. He works his way into the guard's opposite pocket and finds a key. It's an act of leverage and contortion to get the key into the first handcuff, but Billy, always a determined and conscientious worker, ultimately succeeds.

The interior of the van has dimmed to black, and Billy feels himself becoming dangerously lightheaded. It takes some time to work out the combination of locks and levers that keep the rear door shut, but the patient Billy manages. He takes his first step outside and inhales a mouthful of smoke. He gags and wipes his watering eyes. He pulls the jumper over his face, hooking the collar on his ears so it will stay in place.

There are no cars on the road that he can see through the haze and he thinks he can feel the heat from the approaching fire. He glances into the van and realizes that if he leaves the guards where they are, they might die. Crawling back into the van, he tugs one guard out by his shoulders and then the other. He lays them side by side on the ground and watches their chests rise and fall. It's not perfect – they're at risk for smoke inhalation or worse – but it's the best he can do. He grabs the hard candy from the floor and pops it in his mouth. For a few glorious seconds, he revels in the tongue-tingling splash of orange sugariness.

Then, crouched and breathless, he runs away, stifling the immodest laughter of an uncondemned man.

3

"Open the door!"

Rex isn't sure what he heard first: his wife's voice or the key crunching into the lock. All he knows is that he jumped from his knees. He'd been kneeling next to the tub, pushing on the governor's chest in rhythm to *Stayin' Alive*[3] when he went airborne. Until that moment, Rex would've thought it impossible to jump from your knees. If one of the kids in his AP English class had written it, he would've commented something like: Can you actually jump from your *knees*? But Rex had saved himself the embarrassment of ever posing such a question because he'd just learned that you could, in fact, do so. And it's a terrifically painful thing to do.

Now he has to ignore the pain and hope that his respective kneecaps are merely bruised and not broken. The hosiery around his face is making his cheeks sweat, but he doesn't want to suspend his CPR on the governor to remove it. Unlike Urban, Rex knows CPR. He never thought he'd ever use it on anyone beyond their high-school years, but

---

3   The Bee Gees hit was selected to provide the correct number of chest compressions per minute for CPR over disco runners-up *Don't Leave Me This Way* and *I Will Survive*.

here he is, on his wounded knees, pumping away on the fleshy chest of the (possibly former) governor of California.

"I know you're in there if the door's bolted." Sofina's voice is muffled by the door but growing impatient.

Urban places his ski-masked face next to Rex's. "You said she'd be working," he whispers.

Even through the pantyhose Rex can smell Urban's breath and suspects that he had eggs and possibly bacon for breakfast, an odd choice given their elaborate plans for the day. Then again, maybe it isn't the food at all but nervousness and a dry mouth that's causing Urban's bad breath. Even as Rex thinks these thoughts, he wonders why he's thinking them...and then he wonders why he's wondering that he's thinking them...and then he wonders why he's wondering why...

Another rap on the door, which breaks the sequence of wonderings and makes Rex wish that he'd married a more patient woman like a baker or masseuse instead of a persistent and visionary entrepreneur.

"You said you'd be working," he calls out, momentarily stopping his compressions. "You're always working."

"Open the door."

"Get rid of her," Urban whispers.

"She lives here." Rex manages a few quick compressions on the governor. "She owns this place."

"Take her out to lunch then. Just don't let her come in. I'll handle this." Urban removes the ski mask from his face, puts it in his pocket, and shakes his ponytail free. It's an admission of defeat, Rex thinks. The governor is dead, and Urban knows it.

Rex abandons the governor and steps from the bathroom to the living room. "Want to go out to lunch?" He calls in the direction of the door. "We can leave right now."

"Just open the door! I've got a lot planned for today."

Rex returns to the bathroom. "She's not going any-where. We'll have to get him out of here somehow."

Urban looks at him with a measure of disgust, then tries to tug the overweight governor's body out of the tub but without much success. "Help me," Urban murmurs as he locks his hands beneath the governor's armpits.

Rex grabs the governor's feet, lifts, and instantly regrets it. The governor's even heavier than he looks. A dagger stabs Rex in the small of his back and even CELEBRATATE can't help him now. He straightens up and a hot wet burn like flowing lava descends from his sciatica to his bruised knee-caps. Pain is an illusion, he tells himself. He squats again, only this time with a straight back, and manages to lift the governor's legs. The back, thigh, and knee pain is no illu-sion but bearable, just barely, in this position.

Together he and Urban waddle out of the bathroom with the governor's body between them. Once outside, they start in two different directions, at first stretching and then dropping the body. It lands with a thump and a single, heavy vibration in the floor.

"What's that?" Sofina yells from outside.

"I, uh, fell," Rex calls.

"What's going on in there?"

He and Urban stare down at the governor, who's sitting on the floor with his arms and legs extended as if prepar-ing to do a sit-up. Rex and Urban put their hands on their knees to recover and catch their breaths.

"Where are we going to put him?" Rex says.

"Under the bed?"

"Where we *sleep*?"

"On the terrace?"

"Where we drink?"

Urban looks around the room. "The closet then."

Rex can't think of any other good option. "It'll have to do."

Urban opens the closet door. He then gives Rex a what-the-hell gesture, and together they push, roll, and then stuff the large body into the closet and shut the door.

"Open the door now!" Sofina again.

"Coming..."

Rex rubs his back. Urban plops down on the couch. Rex takes a calming breath and then goes to the front door and unlocks the deadbolt. Sofina strides past him, then stops, wheels around, and glares. And it's at that moment, staring into Sofina's wide, disbelieving eyes, that Rex realizes he forgot to remove the pantyhose from his face.

4

Billy sits on a rock by the side of the road, distressingly conspicuous in his orange prison jumper.

A choking wind swirls in his protruding ears and raises the hair on his arms. The sky is dotted with stiff, angular birds flying formlessly and not in the extended V-shapes that Billy recalls. Why don't they fly in patterns anymore?

Is it the fire?

The smoke?

Or have they evolved in some peculiar way like giant squids or Australians?

He's been away for too long. He questions whether birds ever flew in 'V' shapes at all. Maybe it's something he imagined, like so many other things. Prison has changed him, made him doubtful and anxious. He doesn't know what's real anymore. Did he ever?

The prison transport van vanished in the smoke behind him twenty or thirty minutes ago, and he can't estimate how far he's travelled. A mile? Two? Three? The air is asphyxiating, and as he wipes his watery, burning eyes he ponders if this is the day that the fire will find the sea.

"When the fire touches the sea, California will no longer be." That's what they say.

For the last ten years, Billy'd heard stories of how the ocean is rising, the mountain fires descending, and the desert expanding. He'd imagined it all while meditating in his prison cell with his back against the mattress and heels high on the side wall, repeating his mantra:

"Breathing in time.

Lemon and lime.

Rhythm and rhyme."

In this position, he'd envisioned his fellow citizens boiling in the rising sea, pictured his fellow inmates' blistered bodies grilling against the bars of their cells. But now he understands he was incorrect. He'd been thinking that Californians would die when the desert becomes sea and the coast becomes fire – and that the only choices would be between starving, drowning, and burning. But he'd been wrong about that. As wrong as he could be. Californians aren't going to die this way; they're going to live this way.

Except for Billy, that is. He's not going to burn, bubble, or stew. He's alive and free and intends to put as much distance as possible between him and the state that intends to kill him.

India. That's where he'll go. He's read about the massive slums of Kolkata and imagined himself there, pale-faced and big-eared amongst the poorest of the poor, unknown and unbathed amidst the hungry millions, scrabbling for food, drugs, and alcohol. He'd find an Indian woman whose thick black, unwashed hair would be the perfect offset to her large, emerald eyes. They'd have seven emerald-eyed, large eared children who'd beg in railway stations and play on toxic landfills. And within this world of sickness, deprivation, and despair, they'd build a life of love and intoxication. It's a romantic view of poverty, and wholly unfair to the impoverished, but the heart wants what the heart wants.

He looks down the road to his left and sees red taillights, faintly through the haze. He runs in that direction and comes upon a young couple in the front seat of a pickup. He studies them from behind, watching the expression of the driver as he morphs in the blue glow of his eCatt. The woman next to him is extremely attractive but strangely motionless.

Billy hesitates. It's a risk, but as he glances down the empty road and across the fiery desert, he knows it's a risk he'll have to take. He opens the passenger door and peers inside.

"Going my way?" He flashes a winning smile.

The woman spins in her seat. She's bald with strikingly round, liquid blue eyes. "Hi, handsome!" she says.

"Which way you headed?"

"The *weDrive* pulled us over," the man says. "It must've shut down all of the cars on this road. Must be the fires." He has dark circles under his eyes and gestures in a vague manner to the desert.

Billy takes in the faint orange glow in the distance, more for their sake than his own. "Well, as they say in the bar, you don't have to go home, but you can't stay here. The fire and smoke are moving fast in this direction, and we need to go."

The driver looks Billy over and squints. The prison antenna in Billy's head signals that the driver might be a person to be wary of. Then again, almost every person Billy's met for the last ten years has been suspicious. He scans for tattoos but finds none and no visible bruises either.

"The hell you come from anyway?" the driver says.

"My car was automatically shut down too."

"Don't see no car."

"Back there," Billy points vaguely, "Off road. In the desert."

"Call SpeedyDrone. They can help." The driver says, rubbing his thick neck. He leans over the woman to pull the passenger door shut. "Is that a prison jumper?" he says, beady eyes popping. "Wait, are you that killer dude? Who was going to be executed? I was just watching something about you. You escaped?"

He holds out his eCatt so Billy can see himself, looking sinister and floppy eared in a ten year old mug shot. Billy counters this image with mock humility and a winning smile, the one he used whenever he wanted an extra raisin in his prison oatmeal.

"I guess I did," he says.

It's a quick decision for him and an unusual one. Honesty doesn't come easily, not since his trial. Being a suspected cannibal can be a conversation stopper, even in prison.[4] So Billy had gotten into the habit of not admitting his name or alleged crimes to anyone, even to the guards. Still, there seems no point in denying it now, alone on the highway, in his orange prison jumper and speaking to the only people who can save him.

"They said you *could* be innocent. That's some serious bad luck. My name is Mack." The driver nods respectfully. "This here is Sally. Say hi, Sally"

---

4   Though one inmate persisted in asking whether Billy had eaten human flesh, "with salt, ketchup, mustard or any of that other condiment shit."

"Hello there!" Her voice is the ideal mix of bluesy and sweet. She blinks coyly at Billy and shrugs her shoulders back and forth in a cute, little dance.

Billy takes these introductions as an invitation of sorts. "Can you override the *weDrive*?"

He thinks that Sally sure would've made an ideal cell-mate with her sculpted breasts and wet blue eyes. Even her hairlessness is attractive. Billy'd heard in prison that you were now more likely to find a young woman wearing eye-glasses than having hair and didn't believe it until now. "Can you drive us away from here?"

"Ain't legal to be on the road with these big fires unless it's an emergency," Mack says.

"If we get stopped, you can tell them I forced you to do it. What's the point of being an alleged serial killer if you can't make people do things?" Billy laughs in what he hopes is a harmless manner.

"We'd have to head south to the city," Mack says. "Gets real dark, real quick the other way. Hot too."

"Let's head for the bridge then," Billy says as if he's one of them, as if they've been travelling together all along. They seem awfully friendly, and he wonders if people have grown more trusting since he's been away. Maybe it's all the surveillance he's been reading about, or just that everything is speeding up, even the time it takes to trust someone. No matter what, he's in luck.

Mack puts an arm around Sally's waist and slides her over. Billy slips into the vacated space like an old friend. Mack disengages the *weDrive* and takes the wheel in his own hands. "Gonna have to steer." He sinks deeper into the seat. "Haven't done that in years."

Billy's arm rubs against Sally's, and he smiles. Her skin is smooth and cushiony, as if she's just rubbed soft leather into her flesh.

"You're cute!" she says.

"She's a charmer, this one," Mack says. "Better than the last one."

Mack snaps on the headlights and the truck begins tunneling through the smoke. Billy lets himself relax for the first time in days. He tilts his head back and imagines these two are like the family he never had, a brother and a sister, looking out for one another, united and uncomplicated and on their way. They want nothing more than to help him. Billy swallows hard and his eyes water. This is what he missed in prison. This is what he'd longed for: kind people without expectation, friendly people without destination.

He stares at the highway sliding beneath the hood of the truck and marvels at how much has changed in the last hour or so. He was on his way to be executed, should even be dead by now, instead of barreling down the empty highway. He'd like to take a quick nap, but sleep is like a little death as someone once said. And he was close enough to that already. These two seem trustworthy but who knows.

A few more miles and the smoke starts to lift. In the distance, Billy spies the fat stanchions of the Golden Gate Bridge. And on the other side of the bridge, the city, ghost-like and indomitable, the jubilant haunt of hippies, foodies, and techies, of mystics and statistics. To Billy, it seems too easy: the fires and floods, his escape, his good fortune in finding Mack and Sally. Then again, after ten years inside, he's due for a run of good luck. Maybe fortune is smiling on Billy Wharton for the first time. There's an odd swell of emotions within him, feelings he can no longer identify having to do with awe and faith and glee.

He turns and looks out the truck's rear window. There's nobody following them. He's as infamous as a man can be, the emblem of Governor Abbot Swenson's law-and-order emphasis, and the police will use every resource at hand to recapture him. But they haven't found him yet. He's aware that he has a biochip embedded somewhere in his body, so they won't have trouble locating him. But he hopes that with the fires and floods, and if he keeps moving, and is well disguised, he'll have at least a few hours head start. Maybe, just maybe, that'll be enough.

He knows most men get tired of running and eventually turn themselves in if only to maintain their sanity and get a good night's sleep. But Billy's not like most men, and he has things to do. He'll make love to a willing woman for one, and then smoke some pot and drink some wine, before subsisting merrily in a Kolkata slum. For he's Billy Wharton, after all, vegetarian, jailhouse meditator, and animal rescuer – a free man who intends to stay that way.

"I wonder if I could borrow your clothes," he says.

"Sure, but I'm a lot bigger than you," Mack says.

"I meant Sally's clothes."

She smiles.

5

Though Urban prides himself on being infallibly well-mannered for a rootless surfer, he didn't rise to greet Sofina when she marched into the room.

He believes an exception is acceptable in this case, having recently stuffed a dead body into her closet. He privately compliments himself on the impressive job he's done of sitting elegantly on the couch and never once glancing in the direction of the closet. Not that he doesn't feel the impulse in order to make sure that there's no hair or clothing protruding from the door, but he'll resist. He's better than that.

There'll be more he needs to resist, like thoughts about the fact that he killed a man. Even if it was an accident and that man was dangerous and despicable, he was a human being. That's something that Urban will have to come to terms with eventually.

Sofina drops down next to him, kicks off her shoes, and runs a hand over her hairless head. As she curls her tiny feet beneath her, he can't resist glancing down. Her flawless toes have the polish of ocean stones, and he's always pleased when he can glimpse them. Rex's a lucky man in that regard; Sofina's pretty feet are a treasure – as is the fact that she sold her company for umpteen billion EuroDollars.

She's already poured herself a glass of Hair of the Bog Irish tea[5] but didn't offer him any, so it's as if she's lost her manners as well. Manners are the tethers to civilization and, if so, a degree of nastiness and brutishness has already entered this penthouse.

The good thing is that Sofina no longer seems to care why Rex was wearing pantyhose over his face when she arrived. She's a formidable woman, who always gets what she wants, so Rex would've been in trouble there. At least, Rex has since had the good sense to remove the pantyhose from his head. But in his increasing nervousness, he's stretched the nylon over his left hand, made a mouth between his thumb and forefinger and in a funny voice has started saying stupid things like, "Boy, these leggings are handy!" and "Do these nylons make my thumb look fat?" Urban sees the thin red line on the bottom of Rex's neck where the pantyhose were tighter and thinks Rex looks like he just survived a rough session of auto-erotic asphyxiation. Which might be what Sofina is thinking too.

"Will you be leaving soon?" she asks him. She tilts her bald head back as a swig of tea bobs down her throat.

Rex has begun calling his hand puppet Mr. Thumbster, and Urban knows he has a decision to make. Sofina's commands are often disguised as questions – a quirk of the rich and powerful – and this is no exception. She's telling him to go. But Rex seems increasingly unstable, and Urban knows that Rex likely can't handle the burden of keeping a dead body in his closet for long. Not by himself. His hand puppetry indicates that the governor's death is weighing heavily on his mind. Rex's always suffered from an excess of

---

5   'It's peaty fresh!' is the brand's tagline.

guilt and honesty, which explains why he needs so many prescriptions.

On the other hand, Urban needs to get out of the penthouse to clear his own mind and do the hard thinking that has to be done. Right now the most important task is to get the body out, and he can't think about how to do that with Sofina and her feet right next to him and Rex's increasingly antic behavior. He can't just pull a body out of the closet, drag it through the hallway, hold it in the elevator, and walk with it on the street to a crematorium. If nothing else, he has to leave in order to get some body-transporting supplies.

There's a bag for his Takayama surfboard hanging from the ceiling of his VW van that's parked a block away. Then again, the Takayama's bag is thin and the governor is quite large, so it's doubtful that he'd fit.

How Urban would love to be lounging in his van right now, his bare feet hanging out the back door, a cold IPA in his hand. He'd bought that old van because it was, one, precisely what a vagabond surfer should drive and, two, not a theft risk. It has 450,000 miles, a new transmission, a small refrigerator, an old George Foreman grill for cooking insects, as well as a bed and solar shower – all anyone would ever need to cruise up and down the coast, chasing the undiscovered breaks that the rising ocean has created.

He'd been living in that van for over fifteen years, ever since the day he abandoned the law and the lawyering in an exhausted and exasperated state, having worked death-penalty appeals for over 11 years. There are two men who are alive today because of him – though any other lawyer could have done equally as well once the exculpatory DNA evidence came back. He wasn't, isn't, essential, which, for sanity's sake, is essential to know.

He'd grown tired of the appeals, depos, briefs, lies, high stakes and stress, as well as the extension of injustice to everyone involved, the victims, perps, witnesses, cops, lawyers, judges, and families. He'd watched too, too many die due to bad luck, incompetence, or plain, dumb meanness. Every life lost had scarred his heart. Maybe that's why he didn't feel anything about the governor's death yet. His heart was scar-hardened; there were no tender places left.

When he ended his career, frustrated, angry, dispirited, and depressed, he bought an old surfboard and an older van, and adopted a minimalist, nomadic, insectivorian lifestyle of ocean-view parking lots, waves, fried grasshoppers, and beer.

In those fifteen years he'd been watching the ocean – *his* ocean – darken from translucent to grass green before, about five years ago, sifting into a sludgy, heavy brown. And it seemed, with every additional day, every additional wave, the water grew more glutinous. He started emerging from his surf sessions no longer energized but sapped and oily and saddened.

And pissed off. Mostly pissed off. No matter what he did, he couldn't escape. The condemned would haunt him, and now it was the ocean – *his* ocean – on death row, without appeal, without hope.

He hated Abbot Swenson, the climatic Marie Antoinette of governors, who did nothing as the ocean, the air, and the forests simultaneously blackened. Worse, he'd used the destruction not as an excuse, but as a cause for celebration. If the planet has been sentenced and condemned, then let's go out with a rager for the heirs and overlords. Abandon controls, eliminate regulations, and embrace the Last Days of Pompeii in our own time. Nothing seemed to stop the man. Amongst certain demographics his popularity grew. So when Urban read that Swenson intended to execute the last man in the United States – what Urban had spent his working life trying to stop – he had no choice. He had to make his final stand.

Now, Rex makes a weird suffocating sound as he stuffs Mr. Thumbster into his pocket, and pulls out an uncovered, empty hand.

"Rex, can I talk to you privately?" Urban says.

"Anything you have to tell me you can say in front of my wife."

Was that defiance? What for? What's that about? He wishes Rex would stop acting like such a damn fool – the talking pantyhose were enough.

"Is there something you need to tell me, Rex?" Sofina says. "Then tell me."

"Only if Urban leaves."

Urban stares at him. "If I understand you correctly, Rex. Anything that I have to say to you, I need to say in front of your wife. But anything you have to say to your wife, you will only say after I leave. Is that it?"

"You're not my wife." Rex says belligerently.

Rex is upset with him and making that fact obvious to Sofina for some reason. Maybe he's blaming Urban for what happened, as if he wasn't right there, as if he wasn't part of it. Urban decides to call Rex's bluff.

"Okay, bye, Rex. I'll be seeing you, Sofina." He rises.

That gets Rex's attention. "But you're coming back, right?"

"I thought you wanted me to leave."

"I do. I guess I did, but—"

"I'll call you." Urban is a short ten feet from the front door.

"But you're coming back?" Rex's voice cracks on the last word.

Rex is losing it and Urban can only hope that he understands what Sofina doesn't need to know, shouldn't know.

"Because you need to come back," Rex says. "Because if you don't come back. You know…"

"See you later, Sofina." Urban exits and closes the front door.

In the hallway, he leans back against the hall and sighs. He'd always told Rex he'd be there for him, and he meant it. But there'd never been a dead body in Rex's closet before. There are extenuating circumstances.

He takes two steps down the hall and realizes he never has to return. It will be a betrayal, and he's never betrayed a friend in his life. But he's never killed a man before either. The body in the closet will start to stink soon. Sooner or later, that closet door will have to open.

There's no good reason why both he *and* Rex should go to prison. What would be gained by Urban spending the rest of his life in prison as well? He'd tried to save Billy 'The Goat' Wharton, and though he probably wasn't successful, that wasn't his fault, at least not entirely.

And it's not like the governor's death is any great loss. Quite the contrary.

He could leave. Costa Rica has great surf, and Australia, and Ireland, and Brazil, and even Norway. They all have insects too, which is all he needs beside a board and a roof. The ocean will provide as it always has; the waves rolling in through the plastic, sewage, and contamination. One day it will stop, and the ocean will wave its final, deadened good-bye across a toxic, oily surface but until then...

He's never abandoned a friend before, but he's never been in a position like this before either. You have to start somewhere.

6

"Sally, can you remove your clothes?" Mack says.

"I'd love to!"

Sally crosses her arms and in one practiced motion lifts her sweatshirt over her head. She hands it to Billy with the same lively enthusiasm that she answers every question. And now, topless, she points her perfect chin at his orange prison jumper. He hesitates, knowing that the only thing beneath his jumper is his prison-issued underwear, and he doesn't want to have to explain why they're stained. He considers preemptively mentioning the fact that death-row inmates are only allowed to change their underwear every fifth day – TLC Correction's San Quentin prison is a for-profit institution – and that he's at the rank end of a four-day stretch, but the sight of Sally's honeyed breasts and espresso-colored nipples prevents him. He hasn't seen a woman's breasts or an espresso in more than a decade and has to stop himself from staring.

He wriggles out his jumper, hoping that Sally won't look at his crotch. Mack either hasn't noticed or is unbothered by Sally's increasing nudity, even as she lifts herself up from the seat to slither off her URPLE jeans. She flips those jeans onto Billy's lap, mercifully covering his stained underwear. Billy finds himself staring at Sally's round and muscular right thigh that tubes gracefully into her thin green panties. Billy admires the sharp fold in her waist and spies a perfect dime-sized bruise, the color of redwood, on her left knee. It doesn't look quite real, as if it's been painted there.

He fights a sudden urge to lick that bruise, imagining for some reason that it will taste like red licorice. He forces himself to look forward and swallows a second urge to tell Sally that he's never seen anything so beautiful as her bald head, bare breasts, and naked thighs in a decade. He understands what this will sound like and judges that his impulses can't be trusted. He's been away for too long to trust anyone or anything.

What he needs is a purpose, a plan, and achievable goals, like any other free, wanted, or imprisoned man. There was a writer who'd visited the prison and discussed this very thing. 'GPP' is what she called it. (The lecture was jam-packed with convicts believing it had something to do with propelling grenades.) Everyone needs a Purpose, the writer had said, especially inmates. It's what gives you a reason to go on. Find your Purpose. And the only way to realize your Purpose is to have a Plan, which is the strategy that leads to your Purpose. And the only way to accomplish this Plan is to set a bunch of achievable Goals that lead to it. That's it, she said, only in reverse order. All you need are Goals that achieve a Plan that achieves a Purpose. That's why it's called GPP, and it's all anyone needs for a productive and fulfilling life, even in prison. Billy knew that every man on death row needed something to believe in, or else he was already dead. So Billy fashioned a GPP of his own.

His Goals were to escape from prison, drink wine, smoke pot, and make love to a warm and willing woman.

His Plan was to go to India (or another country).

His Purpose was to live as a happy pauper with an emerald-eyed woman in the slums of Kolkata (or another supremely impoverished place).

He was aware that his Goals didn't exactly lead up to his Plan – as the writer had instructed – and that his Plan didn't exactly achieve his Purpose. But he was on death row, where dreams were currency, and he'd just made himself rich. Faith is called faith for a reason.

He pulls on Sally's sweatshirt and shimmies into her tight jeans as they motor down the highway. The jeans are short and a little tight, but not a bad fit overall, wearable.

As the happily naked Sally sits between them, Mack studies the back of Billy's prison overalls where there's an ad that reads: The Law Firm of Holly & Huntsman – We Never Lose Our Appeal.

Billy recalls the controversy when TLC Corrections, Inc., which owned a large number of mental hospitals and prisons, began putting ads on prison overalls and hospital gowns. There was supposed to have been a debate about it, but that never happened. Patients and inmates became walking billboards whether they liked it or not.

"You can put on Billy's clothes, Sally." Mack says.

"Great!"

As Sally pulls on the orange prison jumpsuit, Billy remembers that he'd vomited blueberry pancakes onto his pant legs when they retrieved him from his cell for the final transport. He's about to apologize when Sally says, "Awesome fit!"

"That'll be worth a shitload on Auction_365." Mack thrusts his thumb at the jumpsuit. "I know because old Billy here was going to be the last person executed in the whole United States… the very last one… in forever."

Sally turns to Billy. "You're cool!"

"Yeah, he was going to be the last person in history to die like that. Just like one of them martyrs."

"You're a hero!"

"Something like that," Billy says and studies her bald head. He's seen plenty in his ten years in prison, but never one so tattoo-, lice-, scar-, stud-, blemish-, bruise-, and dent-free.

Until that moment, Billy'd been considering ways to throw Mack and Sally out of the truck, take Mack's eCatt, and make a run for it down the road. The problem is that he doesn't want to abandon them, his new friends. He also knows that, like the guards in the transport van, he can't hurt them or even let them suffer from exposure. After seeing Sally's flawless head and caffeinated nipples, he knows he's not going to let any harm come to them. He's too nice for that and considers briefly if that's always been his problem.

He needs to get back to his GPP, and start achieving some of those Goals, which is how he will ultimately end up free and happy in Kolkata. Looking in turn at Sally's knee bruise and her shiny hairless head, he hopes that he might, just might, be able to achieve one of those.

"I don't know how to approach this subject, so I'll just say it," he says. "I know we all just met, and you seem like extremely nice people. Given the fact that I was on my way to be martyred, and may still be martyred if they capture me ... I was wondering if ... would either of you object ... if we pull to the side so Sally and I could, you know ... because I just escaped from prison ... after ten years ... and I may never get another chance in my life ... if Sally and I could, like ... do you still say 'hook-up'?"

Billy hates himself for asking the question that way.

Would either of you object?

After ten years?

Because I just escaped from prison?

Does anyone even say *hook-up* anymore? Seriously? What the hell is he doing? His first chance for sex in a decade, and he's acting like a pimply thirteen year old in his second cousin's trailer. He might as well give up on the whole GPP thing and turn himself in.

"Fine with me," Mack says.

"Me too!"

7

In a state of disbelief, Rex sits next to Sofina on the couch. How could Urban leave? Okay, Rex's been acting like he's misplaced his frontal lobe, and, agreed, he probably carried on with Mr. Thumbster for too long, but the whole plan had been Urban's to begin with. If he hadn't gone on and on that "they can't keep doing this" and "somebody has to do something about something," maybe they wouldn't be in this position. It was the lesser of two evils to kidnap the governor, the lesser violence, that's what Urban claimed, unwittingly preying on Rex's life's hidden agenda.

For Rex had spent a good part of his existence ruminating on the cessation of violence. It'd started when he was a shy thirteen year old in Edmonton and was waylaid after hockey practice by three older boys. As they kicked and punched him, they gleefully described the disgusting acts that his mother had performed on them the night before. Face down in the frozen mud he'd wondered: why? He walked home in the snow with a tingling arm and a bloody nose and pondered the methods to stop violence, all violence, from a schoolyard knuckler to nuclear obliteration.

Later, as his mother wiped his face and inspected his arm – and it was impossible for him to picture her, or any woman, doing the ghastly acts these boys had described – Rex became a staunch proponent of nonviolence. The problem was that both Gandhi and Martin Luther King, the only nonviolent practitioners he could think of, had ended up with holes in their heads. Jesus too. Well, maybe not a hole in His head but a number in His hands and feet, which was worse. They'd accomplished great things, but the deaths of all these peaceful martyrs had been violent, the lesson being that the practice of nonviolence is socially significant but personally unproductive.

Still, there had to be a way. Technology was potent, immediate, accessible, and pocket-sized: a WMD in the palm of every person. With every passing day, more and more persons hated more and more of their fellow persons – and with more intensity. So if we didn't solve the challenge of violence, we were doomed. It wasn't the most original thought, but that didn't make it any less true.

Six years later in his dorm room at McGill University, after writing a two-page essay on a short play by Samuel Beckett that Rex believed presented the human condition as precisely and eloquently as possible[6], Rex arrived at the doctrine of lesser violence. The idea was to meet every act of violence with an act of lesser violence, and in that way reduce it. If this idea took hold universally then all violence in the world would be reduced to nothing, slowly, inexorably. The idea was as elegant as it was simple, Einsteinian even, only without the replication, peer review, or mathematical proof.

---

6   'Breath' (1969) is a 25-second play that, on a stage littered with rubbish, consists entirely of a recorded birth cry, then amplified inhaling and exhaling, and then a second identical cry.

Today's kidnapping, torturing, and accidental murder notwithstanding, Rex would have considered himself more of a preacher than a practitioner of diminishing violence, a man of his do-no-harm ivory tower and sustaining pharmaceuticals. But it seems that his long-held doctrine had made him susceptible to suggestion, and that's why, when Urban approached him with the plan to stop an execution, he was unable to resist.

So here he is, an assassin with his wife's heels on his lap and the governor's dead body in the closet. His hands find her toes, and he pushes and pulls them one by one until they crack, just the way she likes it.

"Why are you home so early?" he asks.

"It's unbelievable what goes on in that office. There are mandatory evacuations in the mountains and plains due to the fires, flood warnings in all low-lying areas, and the governor insists that last execution in the United States should *still* be done. I tried to intervene but couldn't even make contact with him. I'm done with him."

He massages her calves, alternately sliding his hands from ankle to knee until the underlying muscles loosen.

"After we evacuated the Sacramento offices and Swenson declared a statewide state of emergency to suspend all non-essential services except for that damn execution, he disappeared. He was supposed to be at a meeting here this morning, in San Francisco, believe it or not, but he didn't show. We can't have a man like that running the state, can we?"

"Not anymore."

Rex feels the lower half of his jaw become unhinged like a poorly animated character. He's experienced this separating-jaw feeling before, and he knows how to make it stop. The problem is that it will require another pill, and he'll have to go to the bathroom to get it. What if Sofina decides to get something out of the closet when he's gone? That's a risk he'll have to take if he doesn't want to lose his lower jaw.

"Don't move," he says, taking her ankles from his lap and placing them lightly on the couch. "Not a twitch."

"I'm not going anywhere, believe me." She lifts the glass of tea she has been nursing since she arrived. "I'm going to take a few minutes to relax, and then I have something important to tell you."

In the bathroom, he's about to open the medicine cabinet when he sees it: the Taser like a poised, venomous creature on the floor of the tub. Didn't Urban take it with him? How did they forget? What if Sofina saw it? How would he explain it? This is the reason men go to jail; they abandon evidence in plain sight.

He wonders what to do. He lifts his leg over the edge of the tub and is about to smash it with his heel when he stops. He can't be certain that he won't be zapped himself if he does that. He knows nothing about electricity. He isn't even sure if a Taser uses electricity. Can he flush it down the toilet? No, it's too long and could electrocute him.

He picks it up with two fingers on the handle. Then he steps on the toilet seat and places the Taser on top of the medicine cabinet where it can't be seen. He flushes the toilet for no reason and returns to the living room and Sofina before remembering that he forgot to take his pill.

"Get yourself something to drink," she says from the couch. "We need to talk."

She means tea or water, but Rex hears the welcomed knock of opportunity. He goes to the bar and pours himself a generous portion of whiskey, which almost looks like tea if you don't look too closely. He takes a quick gulp to calm his nerves and then refills the glass. He feels better already. He returns to the couch, lifts Sofina's ankles, kisses the left one, then slides beneath them, placing her pretty ankles onto his lap once again.

"A correction needs to be made in our politics and in this state," she says. "And I'm the one to do it."

He wants to respond but is afraid that, if he does, his lower jaw will fall from his face. In addition, there is a dull ache in his knees from when he jumped up from the floor and the pain in his lower back is returning. He needs to get that pill. He'll have to find another reason, and the only one he can think of is that he forgot to wipe, which he refuses to say.

"Forgot something," he says. Sometimes the best excuse is none at all.

In the bathroom, he opens the medicine cabinet and starts sorting through the bottles until he finds SUSTAXIL[7]. He doesn't usually mix pills with whiskey, but he doesn't usually hide a dead body in the closet either. His hands shake as he grapples with the childproof top. Eventually, he takes out the pink pill and chokes it down while drinking water directly from the faucet. The pill lodges in his throat for a few seconds before dissolving and provoking heartburn-like symptoms. Rex bangs his chest a few times before he returns to the living room.

"I should've resisted even more when the governor started that ridiculous Last Days of Pompeii campaign," Sofina starts. "It's the most irresponsible political program

---

7   Side effects include green saliva, pink mucus, black urine, orange semen, and tar-like stools as well as instant death.

in my adult life and the longer it goes on the worse we'll be. Time is of the essence here. Don't you agree?"

"I do. I do agree."

"I need to get him out of office. So I'm going to start recall proceedings for a new election, in which I'm going to run for governor. I've invited the attorney general over to sign the papers."

"Wait. You're going to run for governor?"

"That's right. As soon as I can get enough signatures to recall Swenson's election."

"And the attorney general, she's ... she's coming *here?*"

8

S omewhere between Rex's penthouse and the Pork &
Drones Depot, as he stared at the blackened sky and
the acrid smell of the distant fires entered the self-driving
taxi, Urban knew that he'd return to the penthouse to help
Rex remove the governor's body.

Though the idea of abandoning Rex and the body
was tempting, Urban recognized that he couldn't do it.
Rex was a great, loyal friend and not to be abandoned. If
Urban wanted to be a man of action and consequence,
he had to face the latter of those two; he had to get
the governor's body out of that condominium building
himself.

Now, after striding through a number of the store's
obnoxious holographic salespeople ("What does localized
macrobiotic mean to you, Urban McChen?") he finds himself in the 42nd aisle of the Pork & Drones Depot and sorting through the large selection of hand-tie heavy garbage
bags. It's the hand-tie part that concerns him. Anything
that's hand-tied would be too weak to support the weight
of a large human body. They could pack the body into two
bags, one at the feet and one at the head, but how would
they tie them together? And wouldn't that risk the two bags
splitting apart during transit?

He speaks into his eCatt. "Text Rex Nightly: Don't mention anything to Sofina about, uh, anything. I'm at the store getting supplies and will be back soon."

That should hold Rex for a while. He's a solid guy as most Canadians are and smart in his way, but he has his issues, a good number of which are caused by the four or more doctors Rex is currently seeing, all of them prescribing different drugs or doubling up on the same ones. The only time Urban confronted him on the dangers of this arrangement, Rex had responded with a meandering lecture on the unsustainability of the American healthcare system, which segued into an even longer discourse on the gullibility of the country's citizens and the greed of insurance companies, politicians, doctors, and hospitals. Half an hour later, Rex somehow finished by saying that, despite all that, he chose his doctors by the total of legalized bribes they receive from pharmaceutical companies, the more the better.

"It's a win-win-win-win situation," Rex told him, with Urban worrying after the third 'win' that his friend was having a stroke.

Urban pulls his mind away from Rex's problems and reminds himself why he's in the store to begin with: to find a way to get the governor's body out of the closet. He might be able to use a long, rolled-up carpet, but he can't think of an excuse for getting one into and out of the penthouse.

"Can I help you?"

His heart leaps. He's on edge and needs to calm down if he's going to survive this.

"My name is Petty and I'm here to serve."

It's an actual human standing next to him. He didn't see her arrive. He can't remember the last time he's been in an actual brick-and-mortar store and, frankly, had forgotten that there were live employees lurking within them.

"I need a bag that can hold a lot of weight, uh ..." He glances at her badge:

Petty Kowalski Manriquez
Sales Assistant

"Your first name's missing an 'r'," he says. "Otherwise you'd be Pretty."

"You saying I'm not?"

He didn't mean to insult her. He'd meant to be witty.

She glares at him, and he takes her in. Despite her name, she's pale as an oyster, with wide bugged-out eyes, a bow-legged, praying-mantis build, and florescent blue eyebrows and hair – actual hair – spilling down the left side of her head. There must be tattoos and studs hidden somewhere as well, but he decides not to dwell on it.

"Spelling your name like that, Petty, I can't figure out if you're small-minded, an old race car driver, or just like to make out."

"*Make out?* You mean, like, hook up? Is that what they called it in your day? Only with you, I bet they called it assault."

She's sassy, and he likes not liking her, which sort of means he does. He wonders if she surfs. Her matching blue hair and eyebrows bestow facial integrity – though he wonders if dyeing brows and lashes puts her at risk of blindness.

"You have hair," he says. "Most women don't these days." Why is he making conversation with her? Is he just nervous? Does she have some odd appeal he can't place?

"Yeah, every woman I know takes *BareAway*[8]. They say it gets rid of all your hair in, like, a week, but I want hair." She rocks her head from side to side, flipping her blue hair from the left to the right of her head and back again. "So what are you carrying?"

"Nothing contagious."

"Anyone who says they aren't contagious usually is. I know that from experience. I was asking what you'd be carrying in the *bags*, you know, the ones that you want to hold a lot of weight and all?"

He decides to meet her impudence with a bit of his own. He'd learned in his law practice that, contrary to belief, sometimes the ugly truth is the most disarming thing of all. "A dead body. A dead body is what I'll be carrying."

She glances at him sideways, her bug-eyes taking on a suspicious glint. "You mean, like a zombie?"

She begins walking down the aisle, expecting him to follow and, apparently, listen as well. "Have you seen *ZombAcropolis*? The vid about zombies in Ancient Greece? Where slaves are, like, building the Acropolis? Did you know the Acropolis, the one in Greece, was built by slaves? They carry all these huge stones up to the temple – it was a temple, you know, the Parthenon, but not like Buddhist or Jewish or the ones on the side of your head or anything like that. Anyways, when the slaves die they turn into zombies and wage war on their masters and stop building the

---

8   Side effects include night terrors, insomnia, sleepwalking, hyper-sexuality, coprolalia (the involuntary use of obscene words), compulsive gambling, blackouts as well as instant death.

Parthenon halfway through, which is why it looks the way it does now, sort of half-built and all."

He notices she not only looks like a praying mantis, but walks like one as well, with abrupt, rigid movements of her limbs and torso. He wonders at the complex motor planning that must've taken place in her infant brain when she began to crawl or feed herself and if she ever feels an urge to capture small bugs. She catches him look at her.

"Are you staring at me? Well, I'm flattered I guess. You're attractive but a little bit too ancient for me. I mean, it'd kinda be like dating a zombie."

"You talk a lot about zombies."

"You're the one who brought them up."

"I brought up dead people. You brought up zombies and just called me one."

"What are you, like, a *tutor*? Like a teacher of the – what's it called? – didactic or something? I had one of those. He taught me that word and had some weird sinus issue. Kept snorting, and then blowing his big, red nose, then snorting again. How *didactic* is that?" She looks at him, eyes like marbles, mouth a knife-edge. She pulls a box of Xtra Strength Heavy-Duty garbage bags off the shelf and thrusts it into his chest. "These will fit a zombie."

He walks toward the exit, impressed with her efficiency. She'd led him directly to the garbage bags without any hesitation, almost without looking, and kept him disturbingly entertained as well. She's a resourceful and energetic bubblehead, and he speculates whether she could be helpful in getting the body out of Rex's penthouse. He could tell her they're transporting a zombie, and she might actually buy it. It's a risk, but a third person might make things easier if they could get her in and out before Sofina sees. He turns around to find her.

That's when he sees her standing near the end of the sample aisle, recording it all with her eCatt and, presumably, broadcasting his incriminating purchase to the digital world.

9

Billy exits Mack's truck, Sally's tight URPLE jeans crawling up into his crotch as he steps to the ground.

He can't believe his luck. He escaped just an hour or two ago – he's lost all sense of time – and here he is about to achieve his first Goal by making love to a willing woman, which will put him one step closer to Kolkata. He'd heard that life outside had sped up in the ten years he'd been in prison, but he couldn't have imagined how much. He deliberates whether pregnancy still takes nine months or if the biological process has been accelerated too, like with chickens. Stop, he has to stop thinking like this. Has to banish all thoughts of babies and chickens. He'd learned in prison that thoughts have consequences, and he doesn't want to get Sally (or a chicken) pregnant and have a baby (or an egg) in two weeks or however long it takes these days.

Sally's bald head resembles a white pumpkin and the pant legs of the prison-issued overalls drag on the ground as they walk away from the truck. Billy looks back and sees Mack watching them from the driver's seat. Why Mack selected this spot, on the south side of the bridge, Billy isn't sure, but he isn't going to argue. He spies what might be a grassy knoll behind a small hill that could hide them from passing cars. That's the direction they're headed anyway.

The truck is still running, and Billy wonders how long Mack thinks they'll be at it. Mack doesn't seem to have too much confidence in Billy's stamina, though Billy, feeling like a teenager, doesn't blame him. The odor of fresh cut grass wafts through the smoke, and it brings Billy back to his glory days of running cross country for San Bernardino High School. He'd been elected captain in his senior year and was dating a smart and pretty girl that he'd crushed on for three years. He was young, tireless, and in love, and life has never been as good since.

The world has changed a lot in ten years, but not Billy himself, who's been fixed in time in the tuna can of his cell. He smiles at Sally and wonders if she's thinking that he was supposed to be dead by now, which is a mood killer if there ever was one. He shouldn't think about it either because the more he thinks about his own nonexistence, the more difficult it'll be to perform, but the less he tries to think about nonexistence, the more existent that thought will become. You can be trapped in the trappings of a trap.

He uses a meditation technique and empties his mind. Then Sally gently takes his hand. When was the last time someone held his hand? Her hand is warm, leathery, and satisfying. Is that what female skin feels like? It isn't quite like he remembers but just as pleasurable as ever. Is this what it's like before you get executed, when the initial drugs begin to hit? Narcotics as a hand to hold. If so, he hopes that every man who was ever executed held a woman's hand in his, if chemically induced.

"You're strong!" Sally says.

They stroll up the incline of the hill, and in the distance, Billy can see the city skyline. There's more smoke up here, and as he bends over and coughs, Sally applies steady, gentle pats to his back. It almost makes him cry. It's the casual kindness that does it. He'd forgotten what that was like, to have someone care about something as ordinary as coughing. Maybe he's not ready for life on the outside yet, not ready for the courtesies and consideration – or else he has to get to Kolkata as soon as possible where his oversensitivity might be passed off as American sentimentality. But you take what you can get in life, so he fakes some more coughs and savors a few more of Sally's gentle pats, before he stands upright.

Sally squints at him, and the orange jumper falls off of her left shoulder, exposing a perfect tennis-racket–shaped birthmark, with strings and all. Or is it a tattoo? He'd been so preoccupied with her breasts in the truck that he hadn't noticed it before. There's also a pencil-sized scratch on her bicep and, of course, the redwood bruise he spied on her knee earlier. She's chock full of glorious, tiny imperfections, bruises, birthmarks, and scratches, and he wants to admire every one. The sun glistens off the right side of her head as they begin to descend the backside of the knoll and arrive at a small plateau.

"I want you!" Sally removes the prison jumper and smooths it over the grass.

Billy forces himself to look at his surroundings rather than her naked body. They're covered by a splattering of trees in one direction and the knoll in the other. There's a small angle where cars coming off the bridge might be able to see them, but it'd only offer a glimpse at highway speed.

"I don't have a condom," he says.

"I can't get pregnant!"

"And I haven't had sex with another person in more than ten years. I've heard there's a statute of limitation on STDs though." He smiles in his most charming way.

"I can't get STDs!" She pats the jumpsuit beside her, tapping the 'Holly' in the Holly & Huntsman advertisement.

He removes his sweatshirt and then, ignoring the cramping in his left thigh, carefully takes off his stained underwear inside the URPLE jeans so she can't see them. He lies down next to Sally and begins kissing the birthmark on her shoulder. But her skin doesn't feel quite right, like a combination of plastic and suede or some sort of soft marble, if that exists. He looks into her wet blue eyes and spies a certain lifelessness, as if she's been drugged, or worse. They glisten, sure, and even seem to smile, but seem to be lacking in animation or intelligence.

"Since this is our first time, do you want me to stay silent, moan, gasp, or state random facts? You can choose!"

He can choose? Choose what? He's not sure exactly, and so repeats the last thing she said. "Uh, random facts?"

"Great!"

She begins to kiss him, and then in turn rub him, stroke him, pull him, and massage him. He finds that no matter what she does he can't attain an erection. There's something wrong that he can't identify. There's something about her – about this – that makes him feel uneasy and alone.

Is he afraid? Has it been too long? Is it because they're in public? Is it Mack waiting in a running truck? Or is it the semiconscious look in her eyes?

It certainly doesn't help that every time Billy touches her breast, or kisses a birthmark, or summons up an erotic image from his past, she speaks.

As he caresses inside an astonishingly smooth thigh: "Parasites are the most common form of life on earth!"

As he licks a delicious espresso nipple: "During World War I, the British Secret Service used semen as invisible ink[9]!"

He gives up, discouraged and exasperated – though grudgingly grateful to know that semen can be used as invisible ink, which could be useful should he ever return to prison. At least, this isn't a total loss.

He lifts himself off Sally and holds himself at a distance. He looks down and takes in her scratched bicep, her tennis-racket mark and lower, the redwood bruise on her knee. C'mon, he tells himself, this is an extremely reachable Goal. And you must achieve your Goals before you can achieve your Plan. He looks into her liquid blue eyes and, determined as never before, lowers himself back down on top of her.

"Antarctica is the driest, highest—" He smacks his lips on hers before she can complete the sentence. This might work, he thinks, might just quiet her down, but she slides her mouth to the side of his: "—windiest, emptiest and coldest place on earth!"

He sighs. "Could you not talk right now, please?"

"You want me to state facts!"

"I changed my mind."

"That's what minds are for!"

He can feel the moment slipping away. He lifts himself off her again and looks down into her lifeless, blue eyes.

"I hope you don't mind me saying this, but it's almost like you're not quite human somehow."

"I'm not!"

---

9   The man who identified this procedure had to be removed from his department after becoming the punchline of too many jokes.

He lowers himself back down and is grateful for all the pushups he did in his cell with his feet raised on the bunk behind him. He's on top of her and she's warm and soft and everything he's dreamed about for ten years. In that instant, he's haunted again by once-forgotten feelings, anticipation that's both a thrill and an ache, the lost mystery of pain and desire–

"Hold on. Did you say you're not human?"

"I'm a LuvMate!"

Billy pops up and his erection collapses. As he looks down at her, she lifts her white feet and flattens them against his thighs, as if this is what he wants. She's a beautiful woman (or thing) and in another time and place, or if he was used to sex dolls, even incredibly lifelike ones, then maybe ... but this is simply beyond him.

If only he still believed she was human, and she almost is. He has to admit that the bruise, birthmark, and scratch are terrific touches. Very humanlike. Is this what they've been doing in the outside world? He'd heard something about it, but dismissed it as just a rumor, like so many other things he'd heard. He grabs each of her softly marbleized feet in his hands, as if she were a snowmobile or a dog sled or some other sort of Arctic transport, and feels a chill run up his spine as he realizes there is nothing he can do. The desire is gone. He frees her feet and pulls on his tight blue jeans.

"What's wrong?" She sits up in an easy rocking motion. "Was it something I said?"

"I guess I'm not ready yet," Billy says. He doesn't know what else to say. He's more disappointed than anything else. But in whom? In Sally? In himself? The sexual advances since he's been gone? In his inability to achieve this first, most reachable Goal, even if he isn't sure whether or not it would count? Does the sex have to be with a human?

They dress in silence and head back over the knoll. As they approach the truck, Billy wonders why he'd opted for Sally's clothes rather than Mack's. Was it for greater camouflage? Did he think anyone would be fooled into thinking he's a woman? Or did he just want Sally to undress? He doesn't rightly know but isn't about to change his mind now.

"Thanks for lending Sally to me," he says to Mack when he reaches the truck.

The engine is still running and Mack is listening to a CrowdCast on college basketball. "How was she?"

Billy glances at Sally and then back at Mack. "Perfect. She's perfect."

"I do my best!"

Billy sighs. "Listen, Mack, I don't know how to say this because you've been so nice to me and all, but I need your truck to get away. And you guys can't come with me. So you'll have to give me the keys and your eCatt," Billy says to Mack. "You can report the truck as stolen when you have a chance."

Mack obediently throws his keys and eCatt in Billy's direction and exits the driver's side. "I'm insured."

"I apologize for all this, but as you might imagine, with the position I'm in, it's the only way I can think of."

Billy looks from Mack to Sally to see that they understand. He realizes that he's treating Sally as if she's human, which she seems to be in every way but the most important one.

"Also, do you have a gun?" he asks Mack. "They're still illegal in California I think, but I was wondering..."

"I look like some kinda fool to you?" Mack says with a grin.

Billy nods and is about to get in the truck when Mack pipes up again.

"AR-15 semiautomatic behind the seat. Glock in the glove."

10

Sofina sits with her feet tucked beneath her on the couch, inspecting the transparent film of tea in the bottom of her glass.

She'll hold off on this, the last sweetest sip, for as long as she can. Tea is no different than anything else; the anticipation is often better than the experience. Though it frustrates Rex when she delays sex, as she does, and sometimes for days. But she enjoys knowing it's coming, and the knowing is enough. Rex has told her that this makes the eventual climax anticlimactic, but what can she do? It's not delayed gratification that she's after; delay *is* the gratification.

That's why she waited so long before taking Share4All public, back in 2019, postponing their Initial Public Offering until they were deep into the learning curve and nearly all the bugs were fixed. She was in no rush; she enjoyed the expectancy. And that's why, seven years later, she hesitated before selling her shares in Share4All, long after her financial advisors recommended, and collected an extra half-billion EuroDollars for the wait.

Rex fidgets on the couch next to her. The drugs that used to calm him no longer seem to be working. He needs another modification. She's worried, but her worries will have to wait like most things. In her reflection in the bottom of the glass, she can make out the darkened half-circles beneath her eyes and the drying patch of skin on her forehead. Rex says she doesn't understand her own limits, or anyone else's, and he's right about that. An after-work glass of tea and five hours sleep is all she's ever known of relaxation.

"You have to be 100% committed for my upcoming campaign," she says.

"Maybe you should sleep on it. Give it a day or two. What could it hurt?" He rushes his words, and there seems to be something wrong with his lower jaw.

"Every day is another day lost, and we don't have that many days left. Swenson has to be stopped, and I have to do it."

She wonders how much he understands about the state of the state, how much anyone understands. What made her fellow Californians believe for so long that for every job displaced, one would be created, or that there would be a digital solution for every industrial problem? There was no one – not a single economist, technologist, or futurist – predicting how rapidly the changes would come. She didn't see it either. What they all lacked, then and now, is imagination.

What she did see coming, and what made her a multibillionaire, was the dwindling appeal of ownership with each successive generation. The dwindling desire for homes, cars, bicycles, and all the rest. Private property, with its attendant mortgages, payments, storage, and insurance was something for the grabby geezers with the younger, unburdened generation sharing more and more of their stuff. She knew that there were hundreds of billions in items – clothes, tools, and furniture – waiting to be shared, if only a single company could make it possible.

Her gifts are of scale and scope. That's her singular ability, her competitive advantage, provided by her single mother, who raised her in a San Bernardino trailer park. She was a special alien amongst us, who could see the bigger picture, that's what her late mother told her, and something which, in many ways, she still believed. It gave her power and perspective, enough to create the single company that made comprehensive sharing possible.

It'd made her rich, and it'd improved the lives of many, but it wasn't enough, the mere sharing of *things* wasn't enough. While she was toiling away, 15 hours a day, the catastrophic changes had occurred. And now there's 34% unemployment and too many people on the street. The ocean is overflowing, the rivers drying, and the once-fertile inland empire is crusting in a manner that was initially forecast for 50 to 100 years from now. Not to mention the earthquake warnings. They all have to start thinking more broadly and expansively if they want to solve this. If their collective thinking is bold enough, their plans imaginative enough, then perhaps California can be saved, and the rest of the world with it.

Rex goes to the bathroom and comes out with five prescription bottles, shocking her out of her reverie.

"You remember that the attorney general is coming over?" She points her chin at the bottles.

She drinks down the last of the tea. That's it. It's time to get back to work. She's about to get up from the couch when Rex plops down next to her, almost losing his balance. Is he inebriated already? He places the bottles side by side on the table and then rearranges them by height, from tall to short, as if they are not drugs but volleyball players.

"Rex, what's going on with you?"

He stares down at the bottles. "I don't know. This whole week, the planning, the preparation, and then getting *him* here." He gestures vaguely behind the couch then abruptly stops himself.

She reaches out and touches his hand. She's seen this behavior before, the drugs, the confusion, the rambling. It's the consequence of sudden wealth when everything is precipitously devalued, including a person's experiences and former meaning and purpose. She was particularly sensitive to this paradox of abundance, having grown up where wealth was measured in cigarettes and beer.

"The students in the locker room, they've been talking about me a lot."

"You're paranoid, Rex. It must be the drugs. I'm aware how many you're taking."

She slows her speech, hoping that he will acknowledge his paranoia and irrationality. He switches the order of the bottles, from short to tall.

"Don't you remember when you were that age?" she says. "They're just young students. They only think about themselves."

"They aren't talking about me the whole time... but I come up a lot."

"I'm sorry, but you're not that interesting."

"That's one of the things they discuss."

The smell of smoke enters the room. She looks out past the terrace to the dark and hazy sky. Another day, another fire, another hundred thousand acres razed. Another ocean swell, another millimeter rise in the ocean level, another thousand doorways flooded. Like Sofina, our planet is an overachiever, whose droughts are drier, rainfalls heavier, winds stronger, and oceans higher than any prediction. The effects should counteract but they don't. Fire and flood, desert and forest, rich and poor, good and evil: these things are not opposite but conjoined, sharing vital organs. So there's hope. One of the twins always survives. It's up to her, her half-alien big-picture brain along with her wealth and instincts, to make sure it's the right one.

"I don't know what you're doing with me," he says.

She hears a distant siren, going away. "If I was with a person like me, we'd spontaneously combust. Yes, you're messed up and paranoid and you better stop taking all those pills, but you're my joy and relief and I love you."

He turns to her. "Let's go. Right now. Let's rent a plane and leave the politics and the teaching and everything else and buy an island in the Caribbean or the South Pacific and never come back. Remember our honeymoon when we visited that remote Greek island and met that couple? He was a fireman from Boston, and she was an animal-rights activist from Australia. We could live there. Nobody would ever find us."

"When the world is more healed we'll consider it. Right now, I need you to stop the pills and act normal. Especially when the attorney general gets here. You have some issues that we need to work out. And we will. But not today. Today we need to think about the children who will inherit this land. Today needs to be about them." She motions to the army of bottles on the table. "So why don't you leave those alone?"

She kisses him on the cheek and gets up from the couch. As she walks toward the bedroom, she stops and inhales a sickly-sweet odor, like burnt pecans and sweaty feet. She inhales again and then locates it. Rex yells from behind her as she opens the closet door.

11

Billy pulls away in Mack's truck and inexplicably finds himself with an erection.

He looks at the bald and beautiful Sally in the rearview mirror. She's the most attractive person or thing he's ever seen in a prison jumpsuit, and he grows melancholic watching her stature grow smaller, the orange of the jumpsuit grow dimmer until she's obscured by the smoke and haze. He considers turning around and driving his erection back to her. It would put him one Goal closer to Kolkata and his ultimate escape, but he likes the sensation of being on the move.

If only he hadn't chosen that she 'state random facts.' What was he thinking? Random facts? During sex? Because if she'd kept silent or uttered some low moans or guttural hums, a few breathy *oh Gods* and *yes, yes, yesses*, then he might have achieved his first reachable Goal (though he's not sure if it would count because she wasn't human.)

Either way, it was not to be.

The trouble with involuntary bodily functions, like erections, is they can't be trusted, unlike the respiratory and cardiac systems that are largely reliable. Of course, he's lucky that he still has that function at all, even if it failed him. During Billy's sentencing, the prosecutor had recommended that Billy undergo chemical castration prior to execution – which seemed like overkill to Billy. He thought the prosecutor's recommendations were a joke at first, but then the man went on to recommend an actual drug for the castration: ASTEREST[10]. The judge scolded the prosecutor for overreaching, stressing that he would have no input whatsoever on how Billy was to be castrated, *if* he was to be castrated. But a few moments later the judge asked the prosecutor to repeat the name of the drug and jotted it down.

(It was discovered during the appeal process that the prosecutor had been labeled a 'contemplation leader' by the manufacturer of ASTEREST and had received over three hundred thousand EuroDollars and an all-expense–paid trip to Buenos Aires to commune with likeminded chemical-castration advocates and meet the former basketball great Manu Ginobili.)

Billy's erection diminishes at the thought of castration and the speed of the truck increases as his blood flows from groin to foot. He's going over 80 miles per hour with limited visibility through the smoke. He realizes that this would be no time to get a ticket, driving without a valid license, no valid insurance, and having just escaped from prison, so he slows it back to 55. Then he lets out an involuntary whoop to celebrate that he's not yet castrated, imprisoned, or dead. Gratitude is a virtue.

A fire truck approaches from the other direction, the siren dopplering into an uneven whoop as it passes. He

---

10 ASTEREST also treats ringworm, tapeworms, pinworms, yeast infections, alcohol poisoning, organ fermentations, acne, warts, and dandruff. Instant death is a known and possible side effect.

grips the wheel tightly whitening his knuckles and begins to sweat. He starts to shake and finds himself unable to focus. He pulls the truck to the side of the road, gets out, and stands on the side of the road with his hands on his knees. He repeats his mantra, trying to calm himself.

"Breathing in time.

Lemon and lime.

Rhythm and rhyme."

He's not ready for freedom. Not if every police car and fire truck will cause distress like this. He turns and sees the grand pillars of Golden Gate Bridge disappearing into the smoke. He'd heard a couple dozen times that the bridge would soon be destroyed in an earthquake or a terrorist attack, or that it would be overcome by rising tides and super storms. But the bridge remains, and maybe soon this bridge will be all that remains of mankind, its pillars poking out from the climbing ocean like the masts of a wrecked ship.

On both sides of the bridge, he spies more of those strange angular birds, flying flockless in various directions and at different altitudes, and wonders anew about their existence. He regards the bridge heights, launching pad for suicides, blanketed by the smoke and smog. This bridge has a Purpose, Plan, and Goal, which are all the same: to remain, and there is no greater quest for a man or a structure.

He too wants to remain, but he'll have to achieve his Goals to do so. He'll need some materials to do so. First, he'll need condoms, in case he meets another willing woman or animate, who won't have sex without one, unlike Sally. He'll also need some clean underwear. After that, he'll have to purchase some pot and some wine. These things he can do. He gets back in the truck and pulls back onto the road.

He wonders how much time until Mack and Sally meet up with the police, and the police in turn begin to chase him. He needs an escape plan. He doesn't want to be on the run for too long, and Mexico is an option, but he doesn't know how to get past the border without a passport.

He'd met some Mexican gang members in prison, and maybe he could tap one of them for a workable route. They'd claimed that there were a thousand tunnels, ladders, and ropes under, over, and around the border wall, and that if Billy or any other convict could find their way to Cabo San Lucas, they'd be well taken care of. The Mexicans had described Cabo – if it hasn't yet drowned in the ocean – as a nonstop party of tacos, tits, and tequila. Gang members exaggerate, but Billy'd gladly settle for two out of three. The problem is that the tacos, tits, and tequila are 1,500 miles and a border crossing away, and Billy doesn't think he could pull it off with the biochip inside him.

The world has changed since he'd been in prison, and he doesn't know much about the new America. The state of the country and its citizens are an unknown. Can they track Mack's truck by GPS? Identify his face from a satellite? What about the biochip? Is it sending out signals right now?

The police may not know where he is at this moment, and maybe it's just a matter of time until they catch him, tracking his body the way track a stolen car. The more he thinks about it, the less time he has. They haven't caught him yet because there's no pressing need. They can catch him anytime they want. It's just that right now they're more concerned with the fires and the flood.

Can the biochip attack him by releasing a toxic infusion or heart-stopping pulsation?

Can he turn himself in under the condition that he'll be granted a new trial? Will that make any difference? Will they care about the months he spent meditating for his alleged victims and their families? Can he plea for an exile to Kolkata if he agrees never to return to the US again? As he poses these questions, he already knows the answers.

He hears an approaching siren behind him and wonders if the fire truck has turned around. He peers into the smoke obscuring the bridge and sees a dim red light growing larger and brighter. He gets back into Mack's truck and waits. In his rearview mirror, he sees that's it's not the fire truck but a police car racing toward him. They're onto him. His right foot goes erect on the gas pedal, and the truck goes busting down the road.

12

U rban reverses direction in front of a ten-foot stack of Recycled, Organic & Excellently Absorbent Paper Towels and sprints down the aisle.

He catches the sales assistant Petty in front of the multicolored display of Zinfantastic Avocado Boxed Wine (Liquid Alcohol) that features a talking hologram named Pit. As the overenthusiastic Pit babbles on about the superiority of Zinfantastic, Urban yells for him to shut up, which makes Pit form an exaggerated sad face.

"You're back," Petty says turning around. She's stocking the wine boxes into a tall, and possibly dangerous, green pyramid.

"Delete it," he says. "I saw you filming me, and I want you to delete everything in your eCatt with me on it." He's tempted to pull a box from the bottom of the pyramid and collapse the whole thing but holds back.

"Too late. It's already livestreamed to *WeUs*."

"I'm a lawyer. I'll sue."

She aims a flat gaze at him. "Sorry, *counselor*, but you gave your consent when you entered the store. In here, we own your words, actions, image, and likeness. How do you think we stay in business? By selling *merchandise*?"

"Delete it."

"Don't have a conniption. My channel only has, like, eight subscribers. I've been trying to build them up, but everybody's so busy livestreaming themselves that nobody cares what anybody else is doing. It's just like high school."

"Did you tag me?"

"How old are you anyway? You're tagged automatically. The store's facial recognition picked you up the moment you entered, and *WeUs* also has some of the best facial and gait recognition as well."

"No one can know I'm here."

"*Hello*? Anyone can know you're here."

She places a bottle on the top left corner of the pyramid and then backs to regard her work.

He's unnerved, either by his situation, having just killed a man, or her confidence. The faint scent of disinfectant lingers as he notices, on the eCatt hanging from her neck, the small green light.

"Wait? Are you livestreaming this conversation?"

"Yeah, I'm trying to be all-in media all the time, like, you know, NoPants Priscilla and D-minus-minus and people like that."

"And my buying garbage bags is supposed to be interesting to whom?"

"Nobody, everybody. Who knows? All the crazy stuff has already been done so all that's left about is, like, just the normal, boring stuff, like eating and cleaning and real-world shopping. There's one channel with over three million subscribers and it's just people watching vids of other people."

He believes it, the way people spend their lives.

The problem is that almost everyone, even a scrawny, blue-haired sales assistant at Pork & Drones, dreams of becoming a livestream millionaire. And in pursuit of that lottery of a dream, she's livestreamed him stating that he's buying the garbage bags for the purposes of storing a *dead* body. That's as incriminating as it gets. If they find the governor's body in Rex's closet or anywhere else and start an investigation, they will eventually come across this video, and he'll be locked away for the rest of his natural life.

It's too much, this new generation. Everything is digitized, livestreamed, categorized, and nothing concealed. All those self-sexies, wet shots, and panoramic homies, and you're not alive if no one's watching. A generation of insects in an insect exhibition is what they are. He refuses to be one of them – and go to jail for it. He strides forward and leans an inch from her face.

"Give me your eCatt."

"Why should I?" He can smell her breath, peppermint tinged.

He takes out his wallet. "Okay, I'll buy it from you. What do you want? 100 EuroDollars? That's an offer you can't refuse if you're working here. Give me your password." He reaches for her eCatt.

"No. My life's in this thing. Contacts, vids, images, everything."

"200 EDs." He stabs at it and grazes her arm.

"Get away from me!"

She steps away, and he grabs her by the shoulders, spinning her as she tries to squirm away. As she weaves, ducks and strides, he wrestles her to the ground. They tumble into the pyramid of wine, the boxes sliding and tumbling down. She's stronger than he thought and holds the eCatt away from him in her right hand. He hears footsteps and voices approaching.

"Security!"

"Kick him in the balls!"

She writhes under him, and he throws all his weight on top of her. He feels a puff on his cheek as the breath goes out of her. He reaches up and pins her right arm. He works his way down her arm and then bangs her wrist onto the floor three times until she drops her eCatt. He rolls off her and picks it up.

"Give me your password."

"Perv!"

He decides he can find a hacker to break into her eCatt and turns to leave the store. Stepping over the fallen boxes, a Security Guard puts the business end of a Taser against Urban's neck.

"On your knees!"

13

Billy's last meal consisted of three McDonald's Big Macs, a Gordita Supreme from Taco Bell, a Grand Slamwich with Hash Browns from Denny's, two orders of Popcorn Nuggets from KFC, Rooty Tooty Fresh 'N Fruity Blueberry Pancakes from the International House of Pancakes, a large bag of Fritos, five Twinkies, an Oreo Brownie Earthquake from Dairy Queen, and a six pack of V8 Vegetable Juice[11].

Some of these items contained meat, but vegetarian Billy didn't object. He knew he'd be unable to eat much just before they carted him off to die, so he took orders from the other inmates.

Some of his more conscientious friends on death row suggested that Billy order healthy for his last meal, having taken literally the advice that a person should eat every meal as if it was his first or his last – especially if it was. He ignored their guidance, but now as he races down the

---

11 Approximate calorie counts: Big Mac: 467 calories; Gordita Supreme: 290 calories; Grand Slamwich with Hash Browns: 1,528 calories; Popcorn Nuggets: 570 calories; Rooty Tooty Fresh 'N Fruity Pancakes with Peaches: 510 calories; Fritos, 480 calories per 3 oz. bag; Twinkies, 135 calories per cake; Oreo Brownie Earthquake, 740 calories; V8 Vegetable Juice: 50 calories per 8 oz. serving.

highway in Mack's truck a half a mile in front of the police car, he's starting to see the wisdom in it. His stomach feels like he's swallowed a barrel cactus and his sphincter is puckering like a sea anemone, and he will either have to let loose in Sally's URPLE jeans or find a bathroom right quick.

He considers pulling to the side of the road, but even if the police car isn't chasing him, they might feel compelled to stop and see what the problem is. And who knows what crimes Billy would be committing by relieving himself on the side of the road. Public defecation? Indecent exposure? Urinary loitering?

He checks the rearview mirror; the police car is gaining on him. He's generally not a man who cusses but barks out a few choice words. His life has been an unbroken chain of unfair events, and this is no different. He's not only *on* the run, but he *has* the runs, when one or the other would suffice for any other man. Sure, he'd eaten two Twinkies, most of the blueberry pancakes, and the entire Oreo Brownie Earthquake, but that was it. It shouldn't be causing him this much discomfort.

The siren grows louder as the police car approaches. He wonders if he should chance going over the speed limit. His stomach swan dives into his large intestine as he realizes that he's running out of time. He needs to go. Maybe he's developed an intolerance to sponge cake, brownies or blueberries. He'd heard that intolerance had become a trend with un-incarcerateds, so that not being *unable* to handle some sort of food, fabric, or smell was considered the height of pretention. And he's anything but pretentious.

He remembers that he'd tried a single bite of meat. That's the problem, right there. He'd long decided that no animal would ever die for him. Accordingly he'd never eaten, hunted or tortured an animal. This last fact was something that his lawyer had tried to exploit at his trial, saying that Billy wasn't likely to be a serial killer since they often started out by torturing animals.

Billy pointed out to his lawyer that, similar to serial killers, cannibals started by eating animals before progressing to humans. Billy thought that since he was neither an animal torturer nor consumer, he was unlikely to be either a serial killer or a cannibal. To Billy's dismay, his lawyer found the argument unconvincing and never brought it up.

So on this, the purported last day of his life, Billy'd silently apologized to the cow and taken a single bite of the Big Mac out of spite for his lawyer, the system, and the life he was about to lose. It was on the third or fourth rubbery chew that he realized he wasn't missing anything and passed the rest of the double burger over to the grateful convict in the next cell. More likely than anything else, it was that ill-advised bite and not the Twinkies, pancakes, or brownie earthquake that was plaguing his rectum.

He ducks toward the steering wheel as a low-flying drone flies over the front of the truck. It stays low to the ground, thirty, forty feet up, as it races into the distance, following the line of the highway. Billy is wary. Is this a warning? Have they tracked him through the biochip implanted in his body? The drone was marked 'Freight' on the side, but even Billy knows that such labelling's not to be trusted any more than 'organic' or 'natural.' He peers into the dark sky and sees a flockless splattering of smaller angular birds approaching over the other lane of the highway. And he realizes that it isn't birds that he's been seeing this whole time, but drones, abundant, skeletal, and omnipresent drones.

He's been away for too long.

Some of these drones must be used for surveillance, mobile watchtowers like birds in the sky. As if, in the ten years that Billy had been away, the entire country had become a giant penitentiary. Maybe in addition to pervasive eavesdropping that had started even before he was locked up, observation was now required. Maybe with the increasing unemployment and inequality combined with diminishing expectations, everyone had to be watched.

In 2024, he'd heard for the first time that the majority of Americans understood they would never be rich. This had triggered a collective depression that only lifted when the nonopioid mood-enhancer, SAFEtyBLISS[12], was made available over the counter.

What's the difference between the outside world and prison anymore? In prison, you can't eat, pee, or sleep without someone watching. You can't read or write or exercise or vomit without someone next to you. He'd heard about the lack of privacy in the outside world, people livestreaming their entire lives, the medical and financial records on display, and the rage of sex-selfies. All of life is being recorded, if not by an individual on their eCatts, then by a corporation or the government or someone else's government. Someone, somewhere saw everything, heard everything, recorded everything. He'd sacrificed his right to privacy by going to prison but why had so many of the free done the same? For what?

Convenience?

---

12   Side effects of SAFEtyBLISS include hair growth in unusual places; romantic, athletic, musical, sexual, and intellectual fantasies; megalomania; narcissism, as well as instant death.

Security?

To save money?

With the drones overhead, Billy knows he can't just pull over to the side of the road and relieve himself. The problem is there are very few retail stores left, ones with actual customers inside. But for once in his life, he thinks he might be lucky as he spies a massive white and boxy colossus squatting on the landscape.

The exit is less than a mile away, and Billy slows to let the police car pull up next to him, its red light flashing. They travel parallel for thirty seconds with Billy staring dutifully at the road ahead, never once turning his head. He stays straight as the exit ramp arrives at an angle to the right. At the last moment, Billy swings the wheel hard to the right and races up the incline of the ramp.

The police car continues straight down the highway, either fooled by his last second maneuver or because they weren't after him in the first place. He doesn't know, and he doesn't care. Not now. He has more pressing matters. He makes another right at the light at the end of the ramp, travels less than a mile, and then sees an actual surviving brick-and-mortar retailer, Pork & Drones Depot, a place where, with any luck before his rectum explodes, they'll have a public restroom.

14

Rex clutches Sofina from behind, one hand hooked inside her right hip and the other clenching her left breast, as he pirouettes her away from the closet door.

Only he over-rotates, and they tumble over the backside of the couch. He wraps her up as they fall, his arms locked around her waist, so she lands softly with her face in the cushions. He pushes himself off her back, then hurdles over the backside of the couch onto the floor. Two strides and he kicks the closet door shut.

Sofina has just begun to raise her head when he flips back on to the couch and on top of her once again.

"The hell– "

He covers her mouth with his own and wedges his tongue hazardously between her still moving teeth. He was quick, the closet door was barely open when he got to her, but if she was looking down, it's possible that she saw the body. Was she looking down? She usually looks down when she's thinking. But maybe if they can stay in this position on the couch long enough, she'll forget about it.

He grinds his hips into hers and moans with something that he hopes sounds like desire. He hasn't moaned in many years, except in pain, and isn't sure the sound is convincing. He hopes she doesn't think he's in pain – though he is, with his aching back and bruised knees. He hopes she's not in any pain either, because that would make this an assault – even if it already is. Keeping someone pinned and kissing and grinding against their will … that's a couple crimes at least. Add to that the earlier kidnapping, torture, and murder, and it's been an exceptionally felonious kind of day.

She mumbles into the muffler of his mouth. He can't make out the words but thinks they're something along the lines of 'get off me' and 'stop.' He worries that his weight is too much, that she might crack a rib or vertebra. He slides to the floor but manages to keep his mouth clamped over hers. Landing on his knees is like landing on broken glass. He moans into her mouth, this time in actual pain.

She whips her head to the side, disengaging her mouth. "Stop it!"

"The idea of you being governor turns me on." Stupid, but it's all he's got. He crawls back onto the couch.

She scoots to the far side, then arches over the arm rest and plops to her feet. "Stop. Now."

"I'm overcome with desire." The words are rushed. He attempts a lusty moan but manages only a doglike pant.

"The attorney general is coming over."

She's on the move, stepping away. He springs from the floor, circles around the other side of the couch and meets her just outside the closet door.

"We can't have people over here if…" She reaches for the handle. He covers her hand with his and wedges his foot against the bottom of the door.

"No," he says. "There's a rat in there. Dead. Very extremely dead. Decomposing."

"How'd you know?"

"I put it there."

"You put a *rat* in the closet?"

"Urban's idea."

She glares at him and manages to turn the handle under his hand but can't wedge the door open against his foot. "Let me open it."

"It's horrible. Even Urban had to leave, and he lives in a van."

"You know what? I have more important things to do." She releases the doorknob and strides into the bedroom.

The moment she disappears, his back re-spasms. He yelps without opening his mouth and falls to his knees, which is a mistake. He yelps again, louder. It must've been all that tumbling on the couch or else the CELEBRATATE that he'd taken earlier has worn off. (The SUSTAXIL seems to have had no effect at all.) His knees throb with the weight of his body on them, but the knee pain subsides and becomes less than the back pain – at least for the moment.

He crawls to the closet, opens the door, and peers inside. The governor is crumpled on the floor, his feet and head raised on opposite ends so his body forms a human 'U'. The smell is rancid and stale but doesn't yet contain, to Rex's mind, the stench of death, which he's heard is sickly sweet. Or is it? The body can't be decomposing already. He sniffs again, just a few feet from the governor's face. It's bad, but yet not the smell of death – unless death smells like sweat and burnt flesh with a hint of chestnuts. On his butt, he fans the closet door back and forth a few times, in a failed attempt to disperse the odor, but only succeeds in bringing it further into the room.

He shuts the closet door and scoots to the bathroom, where, as silently as he can, he vomits. The odor of his own regurgitate supplants the smell from the closet, and he can't decide which is more ghastly. He gingerly rises to his feet and steadies himself. No spasms.

He brushes his teeth and glances to the top of the mirror. His heart races when he doesn't see the Taser that he placed there earlier. With his non-brushing hand, he fingers the top of the mirror and is reassured to feel the Taser still there. His heart slows to a modest pace. He spits, puts the toothbrush away, and returns to the couch in the living room.

His eCatt vibrates behind his ear with the name: "Urban ... Urban ... Urban."

"We left the Taser in the bathtub," Rex says.

"You get it out?"

"No, I left it there for Sofina to find. What do you think? I hid it above the medicine cabinet. We'll have to remove it before the cleaning lady comes, but we should be good until then. Where're you?'

"Detained."

"By the police?"

"No, by the security people at the Pork & Drones Depot. They're saying I attacked an associate."

"Did you?"

"That's not the point."

"What is?"

"She livestreamed me saying that I was buying garbage bags to transport a dead body."

"Why'd you say that?"

"Forget about it. They let me make a call, and this is it. I don't know how much time I have so ..."

"But you're coming back, right? You *are* coming back?"

"I should be able to talk my way out of here easily enough. Nobody was hurt. Is Sofina still there?"

"She's in the bedroom."

"This is your chance to get the body out."

"Are you kidding me? He's too heavy, and my back and knees are killing me. You have to get back here." Sofina enters the room behind Rex. "End call," he says to his eCatt but too late. She's seen him.

"Who was that?"

"Uh, Urban."

"What did he want?"

"To come back."

"Then why'd he leave?"

"So he could come back."

"Why didn't he just stay here?"

"Because he wants to come back, and if he stayed, he'd already be here, and he wouldn't be able to do what he wants to do, which is come back."

She sets her feet to face him and glares. "Stop it, Rex. Just stop it. Tell me what's going on?"

He considers lying but doesn't know if he's capable of telling a believable lie. Because other than understating the amount of prescription drugs he's taking and declaring an admiration for the cohesion of democratic socialist societies rather than admit his lust for the women ex-Prime Ministers of Nordic countries,[13] he's been unable to deceive Sofina in any way. So he's almost relieved when he finds out he won't have to try.

"Because I know it isn't a rat in the closet," she says. "I saw the body."

---

13 Specifically Gro Harlem Brundtland, Anneli Jäätteenmäki, Jóhanna Sigurðardóttir, Erna Solberg, Mari Johanna Kiviniemi, and the lovable and clumsy Helle Thorning-Schmidt.

Share4All
Founder's IPO Letter

*I*t started with a mountain of trash, an enormous landfill of dispossessed goods in the Sonoran Desert.

I'd gone there to discard a few items of my own: a desk, a couch, and a lamp. I intended to drop these items off and go when something high on the mountainside caught my eye. I looked up and saw, amidst the spot fires, oil puddles, and contraptions, a man in a porcelain bathtub. He was screaming and barreling down the hill as if he was in a luge event. I thought he was going to die.

As he approached, I realized that he was screaming, not in fear, but for joy. There was a track down the side of the mountain that was composed of large appliances, plastic sheeting, tiles, desks, chairs, and whatever was available. The man in the bathtub gained speed as he went, and I was thinking that this can't end well. Then he rocked out of the bathtub and tumbled safely into a landing zone of pillows, mattresses, and cushions less than twenty feet from me. The bathtub crashed a little distance away, upended, and revealed a set of wheels fastened to its bottom, perhaps from a grocery cart.

"That looks like fun," I said.

"Do you want to try?"

As we made our way up the mountain, I asked him if he worked at the landfill. "Hell, no," he said. "Don't work nowhere, no how, lady. Ain't no point to it no more. Cuz there's all this s**t don't nobody want, and they dump it here. They sharing it, only they don't know they sharing it. And I using it, and they don't know that neither. So it's all good. Real good. Name's Benny."

Later, as I slid down that mountain of trash in that same wheeled bathtub, laughing, screaming, and thinking I would die, I'd already decided to start Share4All.

That was four short years ago, and now that the time has come to take the company public, I want to reaffirm the original spirit of our company, whose founding idea was on a hill of garbage. Our mission, then and now, is to turn the inoperative and unwanted into the operative and desired.

We will manufacture nothing; there is enough made.

We will possess no inventory; there is enough owned.

We will simply share and make sharing easy. That is all.

Share4All will always have a strong commitment to our users, our shareholders, our employees, and our communities. I and the entire team will do our best to make the company a long-term success and the world a better place.

Sofina Nightly
October 9, 2019

PART II

1:02 PM – 4:43 PM
June 16, 2029

15

The Attorney General of the State of California, Bassia Augustine, briefcase in hand, stands in red wellies, ankle deep in ocean water on the wharf where she used to perform mimes.

She looks around for signs of creation and expression. But the musicians, jugglers, tightrope walkers, painters, dancers, and comedians are all gone.

Have they given up?

Decided it's worthless?

If so, is there hope for anyone else?

Too many people dismiss these artists as unserious and inconsequential, when they may be the only serious people left. The more conventional, caught up in their everydayness, their possessions and prestige, never consider the unsustainability of their lives, the collateral damage. Not that it's entirely their fault. There's a widening chasm between the damage and the doer, the serious and unserious, an abyss where none can stand.

Perhaps the artists have not given up but have been forced onto higher ground by the rising ocean. The problem is they've lost their place. To her mind, a sense of place is critical in artistic endeavors. Even her favorite wordless jazz tunes – Coltrane's Central Park, Davis' Dolphin Street,

Rollins' St. Thomas, Metheny's Last Train – are imbued with place, if undefined.

What happens when a place is no longer a place, when there is no longer any locatable *there* there? What do you call something that once was, besides gone?

A rectangle of dock wood drifts by. Not long ago, these docks were covered with bold, barking sea lions, but they too have departed. The banner flags wave listlessly on their poles and are unreadable, blackened by smoke. There is a faint rotting smell as the ocean slaps over the stores, platforms, and restaurants, slowly swallowing them. The city has decided that the wharf, the once famous Fisherman's Wharf, is unsalvageable. And so it is.

She sees a woman's face in the second-story window of a former fish and chips restaurant. She's an elderly woman with a shock of gray hair and a well-lived face, sipping a bottle of beer. Bassia looks for a way to cross the twenty yards to her but there is a deep current of water between them, and she'd be washed away if she tried. Is this woman aware of the warnings about the recent seismic activity, that an earthquake may be coming that will wash all of this away? Of course she is. Everyone is. This woman must've refused to evacuate and chosen to make her last stand here.

Bassia waves to her, and the woman – a hold-out artist, in her final act – salutes back. Bassia'd like to talk to her but she is too far away. Perhaps there is one thing Bassia can do, one way to acknowledge their mutual loss of art, humanity, and habitable space, for which this woman, an audience of one, is willing to risk death.

She finds a bench a foot above sea level, puts her briefcase down, and stands on it. She removes her wellies and thick socks to feel the frigid water against her bare feet and then sketches a box where she's trapped, the mime routine that everyone knows. The woman smiles in appreciation as Bassia simulates the water in the box climbing higher. Bassia's eyes go wide, her mouth forms an 'O' as she pushes against the invisible box. But the walls don't budge. They never budge. The imaginary water rises.

She'd come to downtown San Francisco three days ago so she could work without interruption. A massive fire, uncontained, was approaching Sacramento, and she had too much work to risk an evacuation.

In her office are a dozen folders on the desk and a hundred items scrolling down the side of her monitor: cases, assignments, meetings, reports, studies, and who knows what else. And in a secret folder in her drawer, the wrongful conviction cases – cases that nobody but the convicted wants her to pursue and that represent the most solemn function of an attorney general: to defend the defenseless, to implicate the implicators.

A pillow and a blanket are hidden in the office closet so she can sleep on the couch, and there's a gym next door where she can shower after her brisk 40-minute morning workout. Her life, like her art, is an inescapable box. Does she work so hard because she's a woman? Is it the job? The place? The time? Or something unhealed within her?

She rubs her hands over her smooth head and looks to the old woman, who gulps a mouthful of air as if telling Bassia to hold her own breath. The woman taking an active part in the routine. The audience becoming the show, the way it should be. Bassia sucks in a lungful of vaporous air and blows out her cheeks. Now, across twenty yards of rising ocean, they hold their breaths, a final community of two.

The need to breathe increases, and Bassia thinks she should've forsaken the law and instead been on this wharf every day, miming the climbing ocean, the burning forests, and the sliding land. Yes, she should've been here, a daily warning, a silent clarion call, instead of doing the beckoning of the likes of Abbott Swenson.

Because at this moment in time, art is industry, preservation is creation, and non-destruction is resurrection. She doesn't know much of God, has always been more of a seeker than a believer, but sees superfetatory proof of His existence in the rebirth, the regrowth of all that's around her. All we have to do is nothing – become doctors of the earth, vowing to do no harm – and spend our days mastering the arts of preservation and non-destruction. And we'll see God again in the rebirth and regrowth of His bestowed planet.

She mimes a straw to her mouth and the old woman does the same, tilting her head back and breathing through the make-believe straw held up.

Her eCatt vibrates with the name: "Sofina Nightly... Sofina Nightly... Sofina Nightly."

"We can't wait any longer," Sofina says. "I'm at home."

"I'm at Fisherman's Wharf and it's about to go under."

"If any two people can save this state, it's us."

"You've never lacked for confidence, Sofina. I wouldn't do this with anyone else. We'll be staging a coup, of sorts. Legal, but a coup nonetheless."

"Desperate times... You have the documents?"

"Ready to go." Bassia glances at her briefcase. "You know, it's not only the fires and floods making places unrecognizable, we can't even locate the governor or that escaped convict, Billy the Goat. It's like we can't find anyone or any-thing anymore, but I'll find you shortly."

Bassia punches the pretend box that contains her with both hands and then a swift sidekick. As the imaginary water rushes from the box, she slides down the bench with it, her thighs, butt, and back making contact with the bench until she is once again on her feet. She takes her briefcase, waves good-bye to the old woman, and sloshes away above the rising ocean water and beneath the smoke-filled sky and won-dering where God, a goat, and the governor will be found.

16

"All I wanted her to do was take down the livestream. It's an invasion of my privacy."

Urban sits in a metal chair in the dull gray Security Office of the Pork & Drones Depot, the Xtra Strength Heavy-Duty garbage bags on the table in front of him. The Store Supervisor, a large, bald woman with rugby-player shoulders, sits across from him with Petty to her right. The hotheaded Security Guard, who almost tasered him and looks no more than 16 years old, stands in the corner, rocking from one heavy boot to the other. The ex-lawyer in Urban refuses to be intimidated. He's done nothing wrong – not since entering the store anyway.

The Supervisor, who snorted when he mentioned privacy, shifts in her seat. "Mr. McChen, by entering our store, you gave implied consent for us to use your image, actions, and utterances in any way that we deem fit. You have no privacy in here." She talks with a pitchy alto that belies her rugby-player physique. "We can and may identify you by facial, gait, fingerprint, iris, DNA, or other recognition techniques. We can and may record all you say and do, and we can and may disperse, broadcast, livestream, categorize, archive, buy, sell, alter, or manipulate any and all of this."

"I'm not upset about what the store did. It's what *she* did." He points at Petty. "For her *own* channel and her *own* purposes."

"As an employee of Pork & Drones Depot, Ms. Manriquez has the right to livestream anything on store grounds. It's a benefit we give to all our employees."

"You encourage it?"

"It's not a matter of encouragement. We're agnostic on the issue of personal livestreaming."

Agnostic? What a choice of words. What if they knew what was hidden in Rex's closet? Would they be agnostic on that? The last thing he needs is a record of him buying heavy-duty garbage bags in order to carry a dead body. Why did he mention it?

"I just want to get out of here."

"You should've thought of that before you attacked our Associate."

"I didn't attack her. Look, how much do you want?" As he reaches for his wallet, the hotheaded Security Guard takes a step forward. He grabs the top of the Taser in his holster but doesn't remove it. "Relax," Urban says. "I'm just getting my wallet."

The Guard removes his hand, and Urban resists telling him to crawl back into the primordial ooze he crawled out of.

"The only reason we'd want your money is because you're paying for something you bought in our store," the Supervisor says. "What we need now is for you to answer a few questions in order to see if we have to get the Police involved."

"Why? Was anyone hurt? No. Was anything stolen? No. Was there criminal intent? No. So it's a nonevent. It never happened. Let's all go on our way."

"There was a physical altercation, Mr. McChen. It's on tape. It can't be ignored."

"I'll write you a check for 200 EDs for your trouble. How's that? Everyone wins."

"Why do you want the garbage bags?" The Supervisor squints as if he's far away.

He glances around the room. No pictures, no windows, no loose objects, smells like sanitizer. He crosses his arms, letting them know that he has nothing to say.

"The sooner you answer my questions, the sooner we can get this over with." The Supervisor taps her thick index finger on the table.

"This is why nobody shops retail anymore," he says, hitting them where it hurts.

"He said he wanted to carry a dead body," Petty says, the first words she's spoken since they entered the room and the least helpful.

"I was joking."

"You think dead bodies are something to joke about?" The Supervisor un-squints and meets his eyes. Is this some sort of an interrogation technique?

"She does." He points his chin at Petty. "She brought up zombies. They're dead, aren't they?"

"Undead," Petty corrects him firmly as if, incredibly, she's offended by his lack of zombie knowledge. "I only mentioned zombies *after* he mentioned dead bodies. I never, ever mention the dead, undead, ghouls, vampires, or zombies unless the customer does first... even though I think we're all zombies these days. We just don't know it."

"Okay, thank you, Ms. Manriquez. Do you want to press charges?" The Supervisor asks her.

"Could we have a moment alone?" Petty points a bony finger at Urban's chest. "Me and the perp."

"I'm not a perp."

"I'll stay to make sure nobody gets hurt." The Guard taps his Taser.

"I'm okay," Petty says. "If you could stay just outside the door, I'll have him stand on the other side of the table and if he comes near me I'll yell and you can come in."

"What will you yell?"

"Ponytail!" She laughs.

The Supervisor and her outsized shoulders leave the room and the Guard follows, closing the door that seals like a vault.

Urban waits for silence to settle before speaking. "I just want you to take down the livestream. That's all."

Petty rubs her hands together. "You know, I saw something like this in a vid once," she says. "It was called *Guillotine Gloryhole*. Have you seen it?"

He shakes his head.

"Okay, so, this guy Reggie is a real-life human being, but he looks like a zombie without a head because he's, like, got his head tucked into the top of a turtleneck. So then this other guy, Declan, thinking that Reggie is a headless zombie who somehow survived the gloryhole, tries to kill him. That's how they execute zombies in Texas. They make them stick their heads through a gloryhole that's really a guillotine and they chop them off. So then Reggie, who was almost killed, wants to press charges against Declan for attempted murder."

"Is there a point to this?"

"The point is that Reggie needed a new car, so instead of pressing charges he just had Declan buy him one."

Urban involuntarily shakes his head and thinks there must be something dodgy in the store's water. "You want a car from me? Is that it? Well, you got the wrong guy. I live in a van."

"Nah, I already got a jeep. What I want is 1,000 EDs to advertise my *WeUs* channel. I think I have something to offer, you know, only I can't get anybody to watch. But maybe if I could do some advertising, like a banner behind a drone or on a sky projection or something."

"I'll give you 200, like I offered earlier."

"Like you're in a position to negotiate. I scream ponytail, and you get tased by Carl."

"That's extortion."

"I'm not sure what that means."

"I live in a van. How much money do you think I have?"

"You said you were a lawyer."

"I am, I was, but I quit. 200 is all I've got. Take it or leave it."

She considers this and then shakes his hand. She opens the door and the Supervisor and Security Guard enter.

"It's all settled," she says to them and then to Urban, "you have 24 hours."

He grabs his garbage bags and walks past the Security Guard and the Supervisor without so much as a nod. He strides down the aisle between Frozen Potted Plants and Heatless Grills, ignoring the talking sales holograms ("Leaving so soon, Urban McChen? All succulents are on sale!"), and heads toward the exit. The large glass doors to the outside world open before him. It's only as he steps into the liberating sunlight that he realizes he never scanned the garbage bags. He's shoplifting.

He sees the Security Guard sprinting toward him and starts to run.

17

Billy sprints across the Pork & Drones parking lot, passing rows of charging stations and dashing between the Teslas, Jeeps, Fiats, old school Citroëns, and other vehicles until he arrives at the front of the store.

He darts toward the large front windows darkened by soot and runs smack into a tall, ponytailed man, who appears from nowhere. Billy collapses backward on the ground. He's dazed as he sits up and makes sure that he didn't soil himself during the fall. He sees the ponytailed man splayed on the ground three feet in front of him, a box of garbage bags to his right.

"Sorry," Billy says, though he doesn't think it's his fault. "Are you all right?"

"Watch where you're going." The man staggers back to his feet. He starts to leave and then he turns back at Billy. "Do I know you?"

As Billy's about to answer, the store alarm starts to blare. Billy thinks it's for him until he sees a Security Guard emerge from the store entrance. The ponytailed man sees him too and sprints into the parking lot, darting between the cars. The Guard helps Billy to his feet.

"You hurt?"

"The alarm is for him?" Billy points in the direction where the ponytailed man disappeared.

The Guard nods. "He's a thief. Can I help you?"

Billy dusts himself off. "Is there a bathroom?"

Billy enters the cavernous airplane-hangar of the store's interior and breathes the cleaner, filtered air. He looks to his left and sees, less than twenty feet away, the sign of his deliverance:

RESTROOM

A few seconds later he's inside a stall, the URPLE jeans around his ankles, and the world is a better place. The toilet seat is ceramic and clean, not stainless steel and spotted. Despite the blaring store alarm, his pulse slows and his mind clears as he sits down and begins to meditate:

"Breathing in time.

Lemon and lime.

Rhythm and rhyme."

It's not just the relief of evacuating his bowels but the familiar features of the stall that calm him: the tight perimeter, dim light, sense of privacy, and muted sounds of other people outside the door. When he finishes, he washes his hands in the sink and then finds himself, almost unwillingly, returning to the warm toilet seat.

He's shaking. He holds his hands out and watches them quiver. This is the first chance he's had to think, and he understands how tense and afraid he's been. The morning meal, the goodbyes, the silent guards, the drive to the execution chamber, the escape. It seems unreal, like it happened to another person.

If only he could remain in this bathroom. A good dog, Internet access, a little food and water, and he'd be content sitting and shitting his life away on this ceramic bowl.

Toilets may be the one thing that hasn't changed since he's been away. So maybe this is where he belongs, an unchanged man defecating on the last unchanged invention, snug in his box, everything he wants just a daydream away.

He closes his eyes…

"On the 6th of April in 1768, a Tahitian girl climbed from her canoe onto an arriving French ship."

The words come unbidden, recalled from a thousand previous recitals: "Moments later, standing on the quarter-deck, she removed the cloth that covered her hips and stood stark naked in front of 400 French sailors and soldiers, none of whom had seen a woman in six months. The captain of the ship, Louis Antoine de Bougainville, was overcome himself, describing her as 'Venus… having, indeed, the celestial form of that goddess of Love.[14]'"

Civilians know Shakespeare; convicts know de Bougainville. Billy knows every word. Here on the toilet seat in a public bathroom, he can see it perfectly: a wooden ship of soldiers surrounded by celestial goddesses, hundreds of them. Their slender arms beating the turquoise ocean in long, rhythmic strides, their syrupy skin glistening in the South Pacific sun, flowers dotting the wakes of their canoes…

Now, as always, the reverie fails to hold. Something always breaks through: a guard, a fight, an obscenity, or in this case, the store alarm shutting off. He shifts on the seat and opens his eyes. He can no longer see the flotilla of bare-breasted beauties, and his mind snaps to attention. This is no time for fantasies. He's only a biochip away from

---

14 Unsurprisingly, Bougainville's 1771 account of this trip, *Voyage Autour du Monde*, popularized a belief in the moral worth of man in his natural state.

freedom and has a Purpose, a Plan, and realizable Goals, all anyone ever needs. He checks Mack's wallet and finds a license and 236 EuroDollars.

He departs the restroom and walks down the aisle in between cannabized coffee brands and superfood stimulants. Ahead of him and approaching softly is not a bronzed Venus but an exceedingly pale woman with fluorescent blue hair flopping down one side of her head and perfectly bowed legs. She stops a few feet away, looks him over and doesn't seem surprised at all by his ill-fitting sweatshirt and tight jeans.

"You're not looking for garbage bags, are you?" she says.

"Wine, pot, condoms, and underwear."

"I like your style. My name is Petty, and I'm here to serve."

Billy regards the starry sprinkling of freckles across the bridge of her nose, the erotically-charged parentheses of her legs, and imagines all the ways.

18

Rex can't believe Sofina disappeared into the bedroom after announcing that she saw the body in the closet and without saying another word.

She simply exited. She didn't comment, question, gasp, gulp, or demand an explanation. What's that about? No one sees a dead body in their closet and then just walks away. She's a great compartmentalizer but still...

He inspects the legion of prescription bottles on the coffee table in front of him. He grabs a bottle and, with a practiced squeeze and twist, opens the childproof cap. He inhales the satisfying aroma of stale air and plastic.

No. Stop. He screws the top back on. He doesn't want to take another pill, had promised himself that he wouldn't, though that was before the back spasms and knee pain – not to mention guilt, regret, paranoia, terror, and worry. It's a lot to ask from a pill or a combination of pills to cure all physiological and psychological symptoms, but modern pharmacology is a marvel. (They say.) He could eCatt Urban and ask him to pick up a bottle of SAFEtyBLISS. Rex's never been a big fan of SAFEtyBLISS – it makes him feel swollen and woolly — but it's available over the counter, which is enough at this point.

Stop. He needs to stop. How'd he get so ensnared in this web of anesthetics and analgesics, treating and re-treating the direct-, indirect-, cross-, and side – effects? By asking doctors is how, but that's another issue. And because he's unable to bear, for any significant length of time, the implacable clarity of sobriety; his head, heart, and fool-driven soul demand relief.

Or maybe it's just disappointment, the gentle heart-break of knowing that the things he loves and teaches – the precise word, the well-written line – are further devalued with each succeeding generation. How can he explain to his indifferent and distracted students that fiction engenders empathy, the womb of human kindness? How will they know that true understanding is impossible without skillful articulation? How can he explain to those who don't believe they need saving, even as the social, political, and natural worlds collapse around them, that it is only by some combination of understanding, articulation, and empathy that they will be saved?

Then again there is one. There's always one: his student Eddie V, shy, awkward, and unpopular, who's afraid to raise his hand because he knows all the answers, and who eats lunch alone reading science fiction in Rex's classroom. Eddie's thoughtful and original, which doesn't count for much in high school. He has a mother somewhere and a father somewhere else. He'll have friends someday if he can hold out. Until that time, he has Rex, and maybe only Rex. Which should be more than enough reason for Rex to stop taking drugs.

Or maybe, maybe, it's that he lacks the full emotional range – or else has too much. Maybe his feelings are excessively constricted and the drugs are a way to expand them, or else his feelings are excessively expansive and the drugs are a way to constrict them. His life has become a simple, unmitigated quest to feel normal. And he only knows one way to do that.

Stop. He needs to stop. Not tomorrow. Not next week. Now. Though under the circumstances, tomorrow is perfectly acceptable. He's already taken a number of pills today, so Day One of his sobriety would be tomorrow anyway. And has anyone ever kicked a prescription-drug habit with a dead body ten feet away? Maybe... but not if they *killed* that person. Not if they're simultaneously imploding with guilt and exploding with the urge to confess.

He regards the bottles with captivation and apprehension. There's a correct order to the consumption of these pills, and he's stumbled upon it once or twice – it'd left him clear-headed, cheered, and capable – but that was last summer, and he hasn't been able to re-create it since. If he takes the right pills in the right order (Is it tall to short? Fat to thin? Bright to dull?), then his mental focus will sharpen, his back and knees will stop hurting, his headache will diminish, and his worries and remorse will fade.

Once again, he faces the singular, multiple, fast-acting and/or time-delayed prescription conundrum. With all of these pills, there's only a slight chance that he'll take them in the right order. Three of the possibilities – the right drugs in the wrong order, the wrong drugs in the right order, and the wrong drugs in the wrong order – will leave him in worse shape. The only way to get it right is stumble upon the fourth improbability: the right drugs in the right order.

"Rex, I hope you know that things are going to be different for both of us," Sofina calls from the bedroom. They're the first words she's spoken since mentioning the body. Her voice betrays nothing, as if nothing happened. "Once I sign Bassia's papers for the governor's recall and my own candidacy begins, we'll be under a microscope."

He looks at the ceiling to see the lens and instantly feels stupid. Of course, there's no giant microscope in the ceiling; she's speaking metaphorically. He knows that. He's not right and he needs to be. So he'll take the pills in order from the low to high bottles, and vows to himself that tomorrow he will stop, hockey player's honor. He unscrews the shortest bottle and pops an oblong green pill into his mouth. As he chokes it down, he eyes the second shortest bottle, as squat and square as a child's wooden block.

"Did you hear me?" Sofina says.

He swallows a red pill from the square bottle before he can think too much about it. Is this a good idea? No, probably not. He needs to sober up by thinking of the things he needs to be sober for: his job, his wife, his friends, Eddie V, and even Urban who, despite his occasional arrogance, has been a good friend and made a practice of reading every book Rex teaches in order to be able to discuss them knowledgably.

"You need to answer me."

Is she just going to ignore the body? Just going to mention it to him once so he knows that she knows and then be done with it? Maybe she's trying to shame him into confessing? He could tell her that he's already feeling so much guilt and shame that any supplemental amount won't make any difference.

"I wonder if it wouldn't be a better idea to wait a little while before running for governor," he calls out. "Get a little more experience under your belt."

"Kennedy was 43 when he got elected President."

"Look what happened to him."

He looks out the terrace window. There's a foreboding in the dusky sky, a thick shroud of gloom seeping into him and the city. He hears sirens in the streets below, perhaps a dozen or more, so many that he wonders why they bother. The red and blue lights of police, fire, and emergency vehicles flash against the sides of buildings, and the sidewalks are deserted but for protesters and rioters.

"This governor is the single worst thing that ever happened to this state," she calls, "And people have finally begun to notice. It's not just the fires and the flood. There was a man who was supposed to be executed today, if you recall, which was to be Swenson's defining act as governor, and now even that man, that killer, has escaped."

Ah, so she doesn't know that it's the governor's body in the closet. That's either good or bad, but right now he can't tell which one. She enters the room and it's either the new drugs hitting his bloodstream or the new explanation hitting his consciousness, but he's relieved. His heart timpanis for a couple dozen beats and then quiets.

"What happens if the governor never comes back?" he asks.

"Then I'm the governor. But why wouldn't he come back?"

19

Billy fills a large 26oz box from a brass tap labeled 'California Red Wine (Liquid Alcohol).'

A bottle of Old's Kool (Liquid Cannabis), chosen at Petty's suggestion from an overwhelming selection of canna products, and three pairs of fire-engine red boxer/briefs are in his plastic basket on the floor. He had to put the basket down because he kept dropping it. There were too many disturbances.

The LED lights irritate his eyes, and the rotating shelves make him jumpy. In addition, holographic images keep popping up without warning, making his head snap. A few moments ago, he'd actually spoken to a holographic sales person who'd addressed him as 'Mr. William Wharton.' He thought she was real until Petty put her hand right through it.

"It knows my name?"

"Yeah, you'd have to be from, like, Madagascar or something not to be recognized."

Billy wonders if the store recognition system can identify him as a wanted man. Is it connected to the prison's database? Will a hologram arrest him? Can he be carted back to prison without a real human being involved? Are there Sally-like animates involved in law enforcement as well as sex? Cold sweat drips from his armpits to his waist.

"Believe it or not, we used to only sell wine by the bottle," Petty says. "It's cheaper and safer by the box. You can't drink it until you get out of the store though, because there's cameras everywhere, so don't even."

He looks through a life-size, singing ketchup bottle at the end of the aisle to a camera attached to the wall. He turns the other way, squints into the animated, kaleidoscopic aisle and sees another camera. "How come the cameras are so visible?" he wonders out loud. In prison they hide them so the convicts don't black them out.

"To remind people that they're being watched. It's like, you know, preventative medicine."

He looks at the shock of Petty's blue hair on the side of head, the constellation of sprinkles on her nose and her oval-shaped legs. Women have gotten prettier since he's been away. "I just hope I'll have time to drink the wine," he says.

"Why? Is there an alien invasion or something?" She seems to take the idea seriously.

"What makes you say that?"

"I saw a vid once where aliens wanted to take over earth only they were allergic to alcohol so the only way people could save themselves was to stay drunk all the time. I'm thinking that's what you're doing."

"I'm not drunk yet."

"Then you're at risk for being abducted. Did you see the vid?"

"I haven't seen a video or had a glass of wine in ten years."

"Whoa, you're, like, my idol. I so wish I could do that. No, I don't. Yes, I do. What I mean is ... I watch too many vids. I can probably go without alcohol or cannabized coffee, but I couldn't live without vids, especially with zombies. A lot of people think they're stupid, but they're not."

"I've never seen a video with zombies."

"OMFG! Where've you been? In a coffin? The thing about zombie vids is that they tell the truth about people like me, normal people, people working for minimum wage – and I'm *lucky* to have a job at all. That's what everyone says. We're supposed to keep our mouth shut and be thankful and all or else we'll be like the rest, lining up for food and sleeping on benches. It's like we've all been turned into zombies by .01%. But the day will come when the workers, the sick and unemployed, won't take it anymore. And we'll rise up! We will. We'll come at the .01% like an army of zombies. And they'll try to shoot us down because they're afraid we'll eat them and turn them into us, which is what they're most afraid of. You see?"

"You've given this a lot of thought."

"Tell you what? You look pretty ice in your woman's sweatshirt and short URPLE jeans … like you'd have to be trustworthy to dress like that and all. So if you want to watch a zombie vid later and you'll share your marijuana, I'm totally game."

"I haven't been with a real woman in ten years."

"You mean, like, sex-wise or …?"

"Any wise."

"No wine, women, or vids?"

"Or pot."

"In ten *years*? Have you been dead?"

"Not just yet actually."

"We're all headed there soon enough, believe me. Until then, you need to drink some wine and smoke some good canna. Which leaves only one thing. Have you even tried recently? With a woman, I mean. Like sex? Because things change. Every seven years the cells in the body completely change, so you become, like, a completely new person. You become a virgin again."

"I've never heard that."

"It's totally true. After seven years, you are. I saw this vid about this stupid place where women couldn't get married unless they were virgins, only they were all horned up, and so it was just, like, bone city all the time. Thing is, they had a rule that if you didn't do it with anyone or anything for, like, three years, then you were a virgin again. So when they found someone to marry they stopped having sex and got married as virgins. It was called *Retroactive Virginity*. Have you seen it? Sorry, you haven't seen anything. That's what you are though, a retroactive virgin. That's so ice, dude."

The box is filled with wine. Petty stops the flow and caps the box. There's a reassuring quality about her. She's chatty, like Sally, but in an improved way that's easy and comfortable, maybe because she's human. He wonders if in the last ten years all women have become chatty, if there are no more shy women.

He should've stuck with one of them long ago, found a kind and un-shy woman, who would've made sure he took his meds and prevented his alleged murder spree and cannibalism. That said, he feels something for this blue-haired woman, something he didn't have with Sally, considerate as she was. For one thing, he wants her to keep talking, to tell him more about zombie videos. She'd be the perfect cellmate with benefits. He could listen to her for a decade.

"Let's find you some condoms," she says. "I get off in ten."

20

Sofina is more annoyed with herself than anyone else.

She looks at herself in front of the full-length mirror in her bedroom and thinks that she should've started earlier. She saw the signs, as did Bassia and some others. She thought she needed to bide her time, to gain more experience. But she didn't bide her time with Share4All. She acted, guided by instincts. The future is instinctual; it's created, not imposed. She should've known that. She should've acted sooner.

Is it too late to save the state?

The country?

The world?

She sees the familiar indentation on the left side of her bald head that reminds her of her mother. She remembers sitting by her bedside, her mother's head bald from the chemo, and seeing the same indentation. Her only true regret is that her mother didn't live long enough to see her success. For it is far beyond both of their imaginings. And had she lived, Sofina would've bought her mother a dozen of those Cadillac convertibles she talked about and more roasted chickens than she could count. For the foundation of her success, the confidence, the belief, was her mother.

"I've got a secret," her mother'd said when Sofina was sent home from kindergarten in tears.

That day, she'd learned that many of the other kids had fathers who lived with them. Before that, she'd assumed that all fathers leave. It'd never occurred to her that it could be otherwise. She'd seen men with the children, of course, but thought it was temporary, that men were always passing through, because that's what men did. When she learned this was not always the case, that some men stayed with their children, that it wasn't just in Hollywood movies, it hit her harder than anything before or since. It seemed impossible to have lost something she never had to begin with, but there it was.

"First, you have to promise not to tell anyone, ever." Her mother took her hands on the steps of their trailer. "Promise?"

"I promise."

"Your father, he wanted to stay with us. He really did. He loved you, so much, but he had to go back."

"Where?"

Sofina had never been home on a school day before. The park across the way was empty and silent. No cars drove up the street and all the trailers looked abandoned. It was more peaceful than she'd ever known, but lonely as well. She wondered if the two things were connected, if you couldn't have one without the other.

"To his planet."

"Are you saying…?"

"He's an alien, Sofi. He took human form to do some experiments. We fell in love. I was here when his giant spaceship took him away. He really wanted to stay with you, but they wouldn't let him. He had to go back."

"So I'm ... half an alien?"

"Yes, you are, but that's not a problem. Not at all. Actually, it makes you very special. It gives you special powers. You'll be able to see things, to understand things that others won't. Also, you have a secret mission. We just don't know what it is yet, but it's there and you can't tell anybody. Not a single person. Promise?"

She never did and, from that moment, Sofina possessed a confidence that others didn't. Her dirty clothes, worn shoes, and subsidized meals weren't because of lack, but part of her training. She was half-alien with special gifts and a secret mission.

Who should've acted sooner. Because now there are hordes in the streets, fires in the mountains, and floods on the shores. She should've done something sooner. But then that doesn't stop her from doing something now.

She pads in bare feet across the room.

What California needs, what the country and the world need, is a new foundation with new definitions in order to find a new, alien manner of inhabiting the planet. The problem is that no one's found a way of doing that. No one's come up with a workable set of organizing principles that don't damage ourselves or the world in which we live. It's imagination we lack, the inability to think recklessly and extravagantly.

Unlike some others, she never resented her childhood poverty, her almost literal alienation. She's experienced things that others in her position have not and her confidence is self-imposed, the only true form of confidence. And this is the responsibility that started from a five year old's belief in her secret mission. Besides herself and Bassia, there's no one else with the money, influence, knowledge, capabilities, and conviction to confront the current problems. She doesn't have the solution, but maybe she doesn't need one. The future is created, and maybe her responsibility is not for the solution, but the inspiration.

She sits at her desk, crosses one knee over the other, and begins to write:

The problem is not only the degradation of our land, sea, and air but our moral and spiritual failure impoverishment.

We need a new enlightenment, a judicious and yet fearless reassessment of our values, culture, customs, and institutions...

21

In Petty's shower the water is endless and descends like rain from a round, hubcap-sized nozzle that's directly overhead.

The soap is green and gooey, and the shampoo smells like vanilla ice cream. Billy swings his shoulders and head, spraying water in a small circle like a lawn sprinkler. He opens his eyes and inhales the scented air. He squishes his fingers into the soapy green goo and laughs. The shower is a sensory overload: hot, cold, tickly, tingly, sticky, slick, fragrant, foggy, and colorful as a fruit stall. And there's no time limit, no unexpected drop in water temperature, no one yelling for him to get the hell out or getting raped in the next stall. A paradise. It takes all of his will not to cry.

He opens his mouth and drinks a dozen thick drops. He washes every strand of his hair, rinses and repeats, then washes his face and giant ears, rinses and repeats, and rinses and repeats, until his head smells like a cupcake. He's hopeful, renewed, and baptized into the one true faith: the faith of the future. The soap glides across his skin, and he sings a song from his childhood about his head, shoulders, knees, and toes as he washes them.

Twenty minutes earlier he'd walked out of Pork & Drones behind the impossibly bow-legged sales assistant with a carton of fine Californian wine, some Old's Kool Marijuana, three pairs of fire-engine red boxer/briefs, and six ribbed Magnum Carta Condoms[15]. Then, after he snatched the Glock but left the unwieldy AR-15 in Mack's pickup, they'd been self-driven by her rusted red jeep to this apartment. He was surprised by the number of protesters and homeless people on the streets, as well as the floods and the burnt smelling air. It was worse, far worse, than he'd been told. Petty didn't seem to notice it at all as she talked nonstop about a zombie video.

As soon as they arrived in her apartment, she'd turned on a 1999 Privacy switch that, she said, was like a time machine and returned the room to the year 1999, undoing all electronic surveillance. He liked that. She went on to explain that there were devices in her apartment that listened to literally *everything* – in order to purchase stuff or provide needed information or call the police or make reservations or a do a dozen other things – but she hated the idea of some perverted robot listening to her.

Then she permitted him to use her shower as if they were lovers or old friends. So either she's the kindest and most trusting person in California, or California has changed. Or both. Maybe it's because so few people have jobs anymore. Or the disasters have imposed a greater sense of trust and cooperation, and they've all become like an incestuous family. And why not? Why shouldn't they be like an incestuous family?

"You all right in there?"

Her voice jolts him from his reverie, his feet slide from beneath him, and he falls to the shower floor. His left

___

15   "Protecting universal sexual rights" is the brand's tagline.

arm knocks over the bottle of shampoo, which leaks onto his chest. From his back, he tries to scramble to his feet, but it's not easy in the curved slipperiness of the tub. As he secures a hold on the handle of the sticky soap dish and begins to rise, Petty opens the shower door and peers inside.

"You hurt?"

He steadies himself and wipes the sweet vanilla shampoo from his chest. Petty smiles through the steam as she flips a white towel over the top of the shower.

"I slipped."

"I hope so. Otherwise I don't want to know." She laughs. "You've been in here an awful long time. Thought I'd check up on you."

She takes out her eCatt. As he wonders why she'd want to watch a video at this moment, she scans his naked body from head to foot. Though he's lived with full cavity searches and a complete absence of privacy for a decade, this is too much. He covers himself with both hands.

"What are you doing?"

"I livestream everything."

He spies the towel at the top of the shower and considers reaching for it but that will leave him only one hand for cover. Incredibly, he realizes that he's blushing. When was the last time he blushed?

"And you've nothing to be ashamed of, believe me." She points her chin at his groin. "It goes with your ears."

"My ears look bigger when my hair's wet."

"That's not all. Let me get a wide shot for perspective." She readjusts the focus on her eCatt. "Smile."

"You can't."

"Is it because you're an ex-priest and naked? That's okay. I've got what I need." She turns off the eCatt camera, then spins and departs as quickly as she arrived.

He rinses one final time and then dries himself. He looks for his clothes, but they're gone. He wraps the towel around his waist and walks into Petty's studio apartment which consists of a bed, a loveseat, table, desk, and kitchen. He sees the Glock on the table. Did he leave it there, or did she put it there? He can't remember.

She's at the stove, stirring with a large wooden spoon. The aroma of pasta and tomato sauce takes him back to high school, when he returned home after a cross-country race, exhausted and starving, only to find his mother serving him a bowl of spaghetti and sauce. She was rarely home in those days or conscious when she was, and it's the only time he can recall her cooking anything. He subsequently discovered she was drunk and the sauce consisted of ketchup, water, and vodka.

Petty spins around, inspects him from head to foot in the towel, and seems pleased. She approaches with a tube of penne on the edge of the spoon and feeds it to him.

"Still underdone, I think. My mother's Polish and my father's Mexican. That's why I cook Italian." She clucks her tongue.

This is what he's been missing, this new world, with everything aromatic, clean, tasty, and livestreamed. There's a part of him that doesn't want to get attached to it, the fearful part that can almost hear the police knocking on the door, telling him this was all just a tease, to punish him with all that he'll be missing when they execute him.

"I'm washing your clothes." She wheels around on her toes and tosses the spoon in the pot from a few feet away. A splash of water sizzles on the stove. "Except that underwear. I threw that out since you bought some new ones. I hope you don't mind."

The only thing he hopes is that she didn't look too closely. "I'm not a priest," he says.

She grabs the box of wine, puts one leg in back of the other, and then spins like a dancer until her feet are parallel. As she strolls toward the loveseat, he beholds the glorious oval of her legs. He rewraps the towel around him and sits down next to her. His new underwear, the bag of Old's Kool Marijuana, and the Magnum Carta Condoms are all on the table in front of him, next to his gun. He realizes that with Petty, the wine, and the pot, he has all his achievable Goals miraculously within reach. Kolkata can't be far off.

She opens the spout of the wine box, tilts it back, and waterfalls it into her mouth. She hands the box to him.

"This is the first real wine I've had in a decade," he says.

"I'm not sure it's real, but it'll do the trick."

He lifts the box and drinks. The wine is sharp, then tart, and then sweet. He'd heard somewhere that whenever you drink wine, you should claim that it tastes of apricots and lychees, no matter what, and he'd always done that, even in prison with the toilet chardonnay. This time, however, he decides not to comment, not to say anything he doesn't believe. He takes another large gulp before handing the box back to Petty.

"So you're not a priest. What's the split with you then?"

"I escaped."

"From, like, the Vatican or Constantinople or somewhere? So you're ex-communionated? I'm more attracted than ever. Wait, did I just say that out loud? Though it's not like it isn't super-obvious since I took you home with me and let you use my shower and cooked you pasta … OMG, the pasta!" She runs to the stove, turns off the flame, and returns without missing a beat, still talking. "The pasta's ruined, but that's okay. You weren't hungry, were you?"

"I had an enormous breakfast."

"Did you ever perform an exorcism? I saw a vid not too long ago that was scary as sharks. Heads spinning around, bad language, green vomit, that sort of stuff. Do you believe in evil? Like *real* evil? I do. It's out there. Why'd you leave the priesthood? Was it because you couldn't have sex? I can help you with that. Wait, did I just say that out loud too?"

She blushes. Now they're even. He's so grateful that he almost kisses her as she skillfully squeezes three drops of Old's Kool into a vaper. He likes that he doesn't have to talk with her, has little need to say or do anything except exist.

"I know we just met and all. But I dope your fashion sense, the whole androgyny thing you're pitching with your URPLE jeans that don't quite fit. And I dope the way you shop. Wine, pot, condoms, and underwear is a solid list. Who buys all those things at the same time, unless you're still into, like, Burning Man or something? And I dope the whole 'I don't really know what's been going on for the last ten years' thing. And your retroactive virginity. That's so ice. I just wish I could livestream it is all." She finally takes a breath, and he realizes she spoke that whole speech without breathing.

"Why do you livestream everything?"

She bites her thin lower lip. "I think it's just to prove I'm alive. You know, all I want to do one day is quit the Porker & Droner and maybe travel and see Hawaii or even Kansas. Be free for a while and not be such a zombie. That's why I livestream everything. If one goes viral or even avalanches,

I might have a chance. I'm sorry I livestreamed you earlier. I can't help myself. I do it without thinking."

"If the wrong people identify me, I could be in serious trouble."

"Like that. Right there. Who says stuff like that?" She hands him the vaper. He takes a deep, satisfying pull, then leans his head back and exhales toward the ceiling; his mind riding on the smoke to heavenly heights as the room warps into surrealism. This is nothing like the smoke in prison or even before. This shit is potent. He feels compelled to tell the truth, the whole and nothing but, for the first time in a decade.

"I'll tell you who says stuff like this. The escaped convict and alleged serial killer Billy Wharton does. Have you heard of me?"

She shakes her head, then takes the vaper from his hand, squints, and takes a hit.

"They call me Billy the Goat, and I was supposed to be the last man executed in the United States just before I came into your store."

"The Porker isn't *my* store."

Within the increasing fogginess of his head, he's astounded and pleased that she's had no reaction to the fact that he's supposed to be a serial killer except to correct him about the store – which is the best response he's ever gotten. She hands the vaper back to him and he takes another hit.

"I was a dead man, but I'm not anymore." He exhales a plume of brown smoke into the air. "At least for the moment. Thing is, there's a biochip implanted in me so they can track me. I don't know how much time I have."

Petty places a small, steady hand on his. "Wait? So you, like, actually killed people and all?"

"I'm not sure."

"If I was on the jury, I wouldn't have convicted you no matter what the evidence was. Nobody with those ears kills people."

For a second, he thinks that he loves her. "I was on my way to the execution chamber when I escaped." He spies the vaper dangling from his hand and hands it back to her.

"So you're, like, back from the dead?"

"You could say that."

"That makes you undead *and* a retroactive virgin." She takes a long hit and squints at him as she holds it in for what seems like half a minute. When she finally exhales, she places her index finger on the triangle of his thigh where the edges of the towel fail to touch. "Know what I think about that?"

"No."

"I think I might be needing new underwear myself."

22

Rex can't remember a time when he didn't think that someone or something was watching him – the government or an alien or his late grandmother – which made it extremely difficult to cheat, fart, masturbate, and nap.

All of Rex's therapists, without exception, had cited his 'strong susceptibility to paranoia.' And all of them, without exception, had prescribed drugs that they warned could have the opposite than intended reaction and *increase* his paranoia. He'd assured them that since his paranoia was already at a world-class level, this outcome was unlikely.

But maybe he was wrong, and the drugs are propelling his paranoia to an interplanetary level. Though at the moment, it's more likely caused by the dead body in the closet, and the fact that Sofina knows it's there and still has said absolutely nothing about it.

It's his own fault. The problem is that he doesn't maintain fixed opinions on any of the pressing issues of the day: the surveillance state, personal armed drones, restricted healthcare, universal basic income, the indenturing of college students, environmental policies, or anything else. This lack of conviction leaves him susceptible. It's a good thing he hasn't been approached by a cult.

And Urban is a convincing guy, even if he lives in a van. Never listen to anyone who lives in a van. That's the lesson here.

No, forget that. Focus. He needs to be more like his wife. She's right. He needs to compartmentalize, be practical and decisive. Because what requires more compartmentalization, practicality, and decisiveness than disposing of a dead body? He needs to stop taking that pretty rainbow of pills.

He flinches at a knock on the door. It's the attorney general arriving early, as attorneys general are prone to do. He can't let her into the penthouse; his guilty face will give him away. Or the smell of the body. Is there a smell? Did Sofina smell something? He doesn't know. All he knows is that the attorney general can't come in. He'll tell her that Sofina cancelled the meeting, that she's sick. No, contagious. Sofina's contagious and no one can enter the penthouse without the risk of infecting the entire city. The building needs to be quarantined.

He cracks the door, prepared to scratch, cough, and look infected.

It's Urban, and Rex doesn't know if he's relieved or disappointed. Is there some part of him that wants the body to be discovered? That wants this whole thing to be over with? He lets Urban inside, sees the bag of Xtra Strength Heavy-Duty garbage bags in his hand, and thinks that they won't be enough.

"Where's Sofina?" Urban asks.

"Bedroom."

Rex spies a blue pill on the floor, reaches down to pick it up, and loses his balance. He shuffles one step forward and three to the side like a traditional Greek dancer before righting himself. He pops the pill in his mouth and dry-swallows it before remembering that he wasn't supposed to take any more pills.

"Aren't you taking too many of those?" Urban says. "You can barely stand."

"They're prescription."

"Be careful."

"*Careful?* Maybe we should've thought of that before we murdered him." He nods toward the closet door.

"He was a bad person. We saved another man's life by taking his."

"How can we kill someone…who was going to kill someone…who killed someone…in order to show that killing someone…who killed someone…is wrong?"

"Civil disobedience is an American tradition."

"We're assassins."

"You say that as if it's a bad thing. There's a moral component to our actions."

Rex glances around the penthouse, his penthouse, one of the finest in the city, perhaps in the country. It exceeds his dreams. There's almost nothing he can't purchase with his eCatt and have droned to his balcony in minutes. He never thought he'd live in a place like this, with the world's goods at his disposal. He's as lucky a man as there is. Why didn't he just settle into his immense wealth, write poetry, and cruise the Aegean in his mega-yacht? Why didn't he tour the world, set up charities, and become a beacon of generosity and good hope?

"I've got these," Urban says, holding up the garbage bags. "Heavy duty. We'll stuff him in one of these and then drag him out like we're taking out the garbage."

"What if the bags aren't big enough? What if we drop him? What if some nice neighbor decides to help us? Or the attorney general sees us?"

Urban circles the couch and sits down, putting the garbage bags on the table. "Why would the attorney general see us?"

Rex looks down at Urban and notices for the first time the small bald spot in the middle of his head. His friend is not the ageless surfer he seems to be. Is his ponytail some sort of overcompensation, a desperate attempt to ward off mortality, something to which they're both closer to than ever before?

"Because she's coming here." Rex says. "Sofina invited her. And she also saw the body in the closet."

"Glad you're finally telling me all this."

Urban crosses his legs on the couch and, preternaturally calm, stares flatly at Rex. How does he do it? Rex wonders. How can he be so calm? Is he on calcium channel or beta blockers? Maybe Rex should check those out. Or is it just Urban's hang-ten surfer vibe, secure in the knowledge that a good wave fixes everything?

"Does she know it's the governor?" Urban asks.

"I don't know what she knows. It was quick when she saw him. I tackled her right after."

Urban strokes his ponytail and looks at the garbage bags on the table. "Okay, as I see it, from this point we have one of two options. We get the body out of here before the attorney general arrives, if we can, or we don't let anyone open the closet door, if we can't."

Rex feels sharp stabs of pain in his knees and wonders when the ingredients in the blue pill will become active. "I've read that one reason they often catch murderers within the first 24 hours is because they're so nervous they make bad decisions."

Urban looks back at him. "Let's buy time then. Let's glue the closet door shut until we come up with a plan. Do you have any superglue?" Rex shakes his head. Urban sighs disgustedly. "Who doesn't have superglue? I have some in my van. I'll get it."

As Urban starts for the door, Sofina re-enters the room and cuts off Urban at the door.

"Leaving again?"

"Great seeing you, Sofina." He steps to the side and puts his hand on the knob.

"Is it so you can come back? Because the last time you left, you did so you could come back. That's what Rex said anyway. I'm just wondering if you're planning on doing it again. Leaving in order to come back."

"You know me too well." In an instant Urban is gone, before Sofina can object.

Rex sits on his hands. How do you tell your wife that you killed someone? Even accidentally? He's unsure whether he wants her to find out or not. It would be a relief, sure, but it would also set in motion a thousand other things that he can't anticipate or control. And they would never let her become governor if her husband assassinated the former one. This is going to bring them both down. He's going to prison, maybe to his death, and she's going to live in the shame of his own making.

There's a tinny ringing in his ears, jangly, borderline musical. He tunes into the sound, imagining he's a drummer in a punk band when he realizes that Sofina is talking to him.

"... I've been busy and distracted, I understand that. But what I don't fully understand is why you would choose to have sex with an overweight, male LuvMate, and one that smells so badly to boot. He's lifelike, I'll give you that. And I know all sorts of people – respectable, decent people – claiming they're having the best, most fulfilling relationships they've ever had with AI lovers, so maybe that's something we can talk about. But it'll have to wait. The attorney general will be here shortly, and we need to get rid of that animate. C'mon, I'll help you."

So she thinks the governor is a sex animate. That's why she didn't mention him. As she tries to go to the closet, he says, "No, we can't move it. I don't want you to ever see it again."

"We can't have it in the closet when the attorney general gets here. What if she opens the door?"

"That's why Urban left. He went to get some superglue to seal it shut."

"He knows?"

"He's big part of it actually. The main part."

"Wait? So there's more to this? There's you and Urban and it?"

23

"Y ou've got to, like, seize the day ... *carpe fishin'*, as the Romans used to say."

Petty sits next to Billy on the loveseat, her finger tantalizing his bare thigh under the towel.

"That's Latin. I learned it in a zombie vid where all the ancient Roman women were lesbians and so the Roman men were forced to have sex with barbarian chicks ... only all the barbarian chicks were zombies. Eventually all the men became zombies too, and that's what caused the fall of the Roman Empire. It's called *Et tu, Bitches.* Have you seen it?"

Billy shakes his head that feels like it belongs to someone else. Or that someone else is doing the shaking. Or that his head is still and his body is shaking under it. Whoa, this Old's Kool marijuana is good shit. Is it laced? He wants to ask, but his tongue swells and fills his mouth, which is suddenly dry as a cotton field. He forces oxygen through his nose and spies a crumb on the table in front of him. It just moved! Or is the table moving under it?

He drags his hand across the table and feels a swoon of vertigo. Is he leaning to the left or is the room leaning to the right? It's all perspective because in the greater cosmic sense, everything is – even the cosmos. He circles that concept and comes to a further understanding. Not quite knowledge, but something even more certain, something that can't be stated, or questioned, or unproved. It's a sensation mostly, about guilt and innocence, that there's no difference. A sensation that he'd been judged to be one of those two things by people who presumed themselves to be the other, but it could have been the other way around. That guilt lies in judgement; innocence in acceptance. And maybe after all the interchangeable rights and wrongs, pains and pleasures, illusions and realities, it was simply his destiny to live in a 6` x 9` can in order to be presented with this reward: wine, pot, and a pretty, bow-legged woman by his side. All things considered, he's a lucky man.

"Oh, I forgot. You haven't seen anything." It's Petty. Her finger on his thigh has morphed into a palm, and her hand has either edged beneath the towel or been bloodlessly hacked off beneath it. No, her fingers are there; he can feel the heat beneath them. The towel tightens around his waist and begins to tent.

It doesn't go unnoticed.

"Is that rigor mortis?" She looks down. "Or are you just happy to be undead?"

His tongue is thick and squid-like in his mouth. He feels the need to speak, feels that he has something important to say but instantly forgets what it is as his squid-tongue explores the furthest regions of his left cheek.

She's still talking. She's always talking. "... We could like get to know each other and all and then go sexing. Or we can just do sex now. What's the split, after all? If you have a disease now, you'll still have it in a couple of days from now, right? And if you're a serial killer now, then you'll still be a serial killer a couple of days from now. So why wait? There's just one thing, I'd kind of like to know." Her hand rides higher on his thigh. "How many people did you, like, you know ... kill?"

He's an honest man, if not a good one. He's never knowingly accepted the incorrect change, cheated on his taxes, or slept with a woman under false pretenses (except for once claiming he was Vladimir Putin's illegitimate stepson). He would've been truthful at his trial as well, if he could've remembered what happened.

At this moment, high as an asteroid and with Petty's hand resting on his increasingly sweaty thigh, he still doesn't know if he killed all those people or not – and is skeptical that he ate the last one. (Though he recalls an attack of indigestion when, handcuffed in the back of the police cruiser, he started to regain his senses – but that could've been caused just as easily by the Jalapeño Poppers from Wienerschnitzel[16] that he'd consumed earlier that afternoon as human flesh.)

She crosses her oval legs at the ankles, and an animal sound springs from Billy's mouth, something high-pitched and bird-like. He licks his lips and discovers that his tongue has shrunk to an inflated but workable size.

"Depends ... who ... is ... counting," he manages to say.

"Say, like, the police."

"Then ... nine, but I think ... only eight. If any." It's getting easier to talk.

"That's a lot of people. If any."

"I'm not sure ... I killed them," he says slowly. "I was off my meds at the time so there were ... extenuating circumstances. I don't still know why they chose to execute me. I think it was my nickname."

---

16 Approximate calorie count: 300 per six pack

"I heard they stopped all executions."

"I was supposed to be last man executed in the United States before I escaped."

"So you're, like, a celebrity and all. You know, you should do your own livestream. I could be on it too. We could call it '*Imperfectly Executed*,' or '*Milking the Goat*' or something like that. People could see us, like, hiding out, how we survive and all about our troubled relationship. How ice would that be?"

"I'm not sure we have a relationship."

"That's easily fixed." She removes her shirt and stands in front of him with her ankles touching and her slender knees far enough apart that he could put his fist between them. Her small, rounded breasts are capped by café-au-lait nipples that, like her knees, point slightly outward. Why do a woman's nipples always remind him of coffee?

She's the second naked woman or animate that he's seen since his escape. He'd heard stories about how things had changed and women had become as eager and unashamed as Bougainville's goddesses, but he didn't believe it. He thought it was just prison talk, something the new fish used to torment the long timers. But it's true.

He cups her right breast and kisses it, savoring the arousing velvetiness of her warm skin, the clean and healthy smell of her human body. How did he survive without this? As she steps out of her jean shorts, he slips on a Magnum Carta Condom. As he pulls her toward him, he glances down at the lovely outward bend of her legs and sees above them the landing strip of trimmed blue fluff, shockingly blue, phosphorescently blue, Chernobyl blue, Fukushima blue, impeccably matching the hair on the side of her head.

"I'm color coordinated," she says.

At that moment, he understands that he's been away for too long, that in that lost decade in prison he'd become *institutionalized*, the saddest of all words. He weakens. He isn't ready for this. She's blue. Too blue. And he reels as he understands that his enemies, whoever they are, have won. For he knows that if he's unable to perform, if he's unable to achieve this ever-so-reachable Goal, then he will be recaptured and executed. Because the only way to accomplish your Plan and then your Purpose is to first achieve your Goals. One leads to the other. It's simple GPP logic.

His mouth squeezes on his squid-tongue, and his knees weaken as he recognizes that he is literally fucking for his life. That if he can't have sex with Petty, he will be recaptured, and if he's recaptured he will be executed. There will never be another woman and no more wine or pot. No more long showers and no emerald-eyed children in Kolkata. He'll be dead.

It's too much, the weight of the greater cosmos on his slim penis, more than it can handle, and so for the second time that day, as she reaches down and pulls away the towel, he fatally loses his erection.

24

In the end, Rex understood that Sofina simply didn't want to know.

The closet, the sex animate, Urban, the drugs, the paranoia, she just didn't want to know. She'd paced and huffed and glared but asked no questions. She checked the time, mentioned that she had more thinking to do, and retreated to the bedroom. As always, she knows what she wants to know and when she wants to know it. It's a gift. She's the best compartmentalizer that he's ever known, a walking, talking travel-bag of a woman. If her marriage is crumbling, if her husband's addicted to pills, overweight LuvMates, and other men (possibly at the same time), then these things can be packed away and forgotten as neatly as an extra pair of socks.

He sinks into the couch. Maybe the only thing worse than his wife thinking he's having an affair with his best friend and a sex animate is the truth – which is saying something. One moment, you're a pacifist, recycler, volunteer for the homeless, English teacher, and epic poet, and the next an unfaithful husband, sex and drug addict, and assassin. Such is life at the bitter end of the 2020s.

He glances to the terrace, graying with dusk and smoke. Outside this luxurious penthouse, across the length and breadth of California, the oceans are increasingly un-swimmable, the land is increasingly infertile, and the air is increasingly unbreathable. And what, after all, are the oceans, land, and air for? It's easy to ignore, if you're wealthy or lucky enough, but you can't ignore the knowledge that sooner or later, these calamities will get everyone.

Maybe he should follow Sofina's example and concentrate fully on the task at hand. Before she left the room Sofina did just that and ordered some appetizers from the Paunchy Pilot restaurant. She instructed Rex that he should pick them up on the terrace when they arrive. If he could manage to do that much for her, she'd added with a dollop of well-deserved sarcasm.

The drone hasn't yet arrived, so he heads to his desk against the far wall. He pulls the drawer open exposing a number of old coins as well as the tattered manuscript to the epic poem he's been working on for a good portion of his adult life. The result: two and a half inches of yellowing paper. Who does he think he is anyway?

Coleridge?

Baudelaire?

Thomas de Quincey?

Right now, there are only three things that he believes in: his wife, his student Eddie V, and literature. But trying to save a student is often useless, even one as gifted as Eddie V – though that has never stopped Rex. And loving your wife and books makes you a dinosaur. So where does that leave him?

At least matrimonial love has its rewards, which is more than he can say for epic poetry. Which doesn't prevent him from planting his widening ass on a chair and trying to create. People wiser than him have said that to love, truly love, is the best of all possible lives. And to love greatly is to stay true – which he has, to both his poem and his wife. (He'd decided he'd cheat on his wife if, and only if, he and a striking Nordic Prime Minister were the only survivors of a plane crash on a remote glacier and had to huddle together in a cargo hold for warmth and survival, a scenario he's played out a good number of times in his mind.)

He reaches out and caresses the poem that nobody but Sofina, Urban, and possibly a literary agent or two will likely ever read. *'Death in Hilton Head'* establishes Rex's hypothesis of lesser violence with authority and lyricism. (He hopes.) It begins with a torture/murder and ends with a communal redemption for all the characters. (He hopes.) The years he put in on it, tapping away on his keyboard and yawping over the rooftops as Whitman would say.

He flips the cover page and reads:

We are but
single notes
in the discord,
strings plucked once,
sound and
resonance.
Hear us fade…

Is it funny? Not yet certainly, but it will be. (He hopes.) Is the beginning too much of a downer, too serious? Will the seriousness overwhelm the subsequent humor? Will the humor overwhelm the seriousness? Is there too much of one to support the other?

But what can he do?

Because as 2029 careens into history, human existence is nothing but lavishly and prodigiously seriocomic. Everything is extremely extreme. It's not that the falcon cannot hear the falconer, to use Yeats' indelible imagery. It's that the falconer no longer exists.

He'd sent a version of the poem to three of the four remaining literary agents in the US who accepted poems and, of the two who responded, one praised its undiluted violence, the other its broad humor. Neither of them took it on. The agent who liked the humor wrote that she accepted poems, plural not singular, and certainly not anything that would be considered epic. The problem, she went on, isn't that the last sizable audience for epic poetry is middle aged; it's that they died in the Middle Ages. Would he be interested in letting a celebrity or an aging heir with literary pretensions claim authorship?

Though he certainly doesn't need the money, maybe he should've offended his integrity and given the authorship of his poem away. Maybe he'd have been able to embark on a nameless literary career. Ghost poet to the stars. Maybe then he wouldn't be covering up his assassination of the governor.

Two sharp knocks.

Rex opens the front door and sees Urban, holding up a tube of something strange in his left hand.

"That doesn't look like glue," Rex says.

Urban enters the penthouse. "It's epoxy. It's used for repairing surfboards."

25

Petty has locked herself in the bathroom.

Perched naked on the edge of the tub, she takes another hit from the vaper. Her clothes are scattered in the other room where she'd left the limp and silent Billy wrapped in a towel on the loveseat. That's one of the good things about women. They can always perform. And it's not like it's the first time a man couldn't do it with her. Once or twice she'd even wondered if she was the cause of it, like maybe she likes zombies too much or watches too many vids or there's something about her personality, which, okay, isn't for everybody. She talks too much, but that's only because she has a lot to say. No reason to get all deflated about it.

She exhales and watches the smoke dissipate above her head.

It was her blue pubes that scared him. Most people like it. It makes them feel like they know a secret. Ever since *BareAway* came on the market, almost every woman has gone hairless, head to toe. Except her. She likes the way she looks, interesting, offbeat, and with a hidden shocker of blue. But poor Billy couldn't handle it. He must be lonely, with all he's been through. There's no way he murdered all those people. He's too easygoing and funny-looking with his big ears to have killed anybody.

She goes to the door and experiences a quiver of fear. What if he's locked the door from the outside? What if he actually is a serial killer and has locked her in so that he can kill her too? Maybe he's squirted a drop of polonium[17] under the door. Which is a bad substance because it has no stable isotopes – something she learned in the vid *Bewitched, Bothered & Embalmed*. What's an isotope anyway? It sounds like a person with a sexual preference for themselves.

She stands back from the door. She suffers from a fear of being trapped – which might just be fear of working at the Porker for the rest of her life. Which is the world's biggest trap. Most people who work there are pretty ice, and her boss sometimes lets her leave early, so that's dope. But the company culls the bottom 20% of their employees every quarter, and they never want anybody to be friends with anyone else, just, like compete with each other all the time. So you feel alone at work, even when surrounded by people. That's the way they want it. It's just a matter of time before she hits the bottom 20% and is fired.

Maybe she's as lonely as Billy.

She needs to change her life and to do that she needs to change herself. She knows how to start. She lathers herself with shaving cream, then grabs the razor from the sink and carefully shaves away all of her pubic hair. She's surprised at how little time it takes; a few careful strokes and she's done. She looks down at herself in detached appraisal and nods. She steps over the small pile of blue hairs on the floor, goes

---

17 In 2006, Alexander Litvinenko, who coined the term 'mafia state,' became the first victim of lethal Polonium 210-induced acute radiation syndrome.

to the door, and opens it. She's not trapped and never was. She sees Billy, the not priest and probably not serial killer, on the loveseat. She wraps herself in a towel, leans against the door frame, and thrusts out her hip.

"I've got a surprise for you."

"It's not you, you know." He bows his head. "I've dreamed of almost nothing else for the last ten years except making love to a beautiful woman. Now that I'm here, I can't do it. The reason is that I believe if I can't do this then I'll die and that puts too much pressure on me."

"No pressure, Billy. Look at me."

He doesn't look up. "We start and everything seems fine and then my mind starts going like the little engine that could. 'I think I can. I think I can,' but I can't."

"OMFG! I never thought. Were you raped in prison? Like, in the shower? Because I saw a prison vid called *Dropping the Soap* that—"

"I wasn't raped in prison."

A mix of tenderness and pity comes upon her. All her life, she's been waiting for something to arrive, when all that she needs to do is go get it. Take a risk. Seize the day. Do some *carpe fishin'*. She walks over to Billy, lies down in front of him, and throws open her towel. He stares unblinkingly at the newly shaved area just above her legs.

"This sounds stupid, so I'll just say it," she says from the floor. "Let's become a couple. Right now. Let's do stuff together like shopping and eating and having each other's back and lots of sex and all those things that couples do."

"Really? Just like that?"

She reaches up and takes his hands in hers. His ears look extra-large from this angle and his eyes are moist and kind. "What I'm trying to say is... How about, like, I love you and you love me? We just agree to it, and then we do it. Like we're abducting each other, the way aliens do, only with love. I mean, I think you're one of those guys who can't just have sex with anyone. You have to, like, *make* love. I've heard of those guys, and I'm totally ice with that. In fact, I once saw a zombie vid where–"

"Can we leave zombies out of this right now?"

"Yeah, I talk about them too much, I know." She rips off his towel and pulls him on top of her. "You only get a few chances in life and if you don't take them, you'll end up working at the Porker all day and watching zombie vids all night. I guess I've kind of been in prison too. So let's just, like, take a chance. You and me. Not hold back. Because if I've learned anything from all the vids I watch, it's this. That love can save you, even in the 90 minutes a vid takes. And even if you're a zomb– . Oh, I'm sorry. I forgot I wasn't supposed to mention those."

"It's okay. It's just that the police could come through the door to get me at any minute."

He grabs a condom from the table and slips it on. When he's back on top of her, she wriggles and places him where he needs to be.

She senses his uncertainty and whispers into his giant left ear, "I love you, Billy. I love you love you love you." It takes a second, but only a second, until she feels him growing inside her like a proud alien's probe.

26

"We're not repairing a surfboard," Rex says. "We're trying to glue the closet shut."

"Have some imagination." Urban waves the large tube of epoxy at him. "You know better than anyone about using chemicals for 'off-label' purposes."

"I don't even know what epoxy does."

"It hardens."

"And if it doesn't?"

Rex groans. As usual, Urban isn't taking this or anything else seriously. The governor's body is in the closet, and the attorney general is coming over any minute, and they're trying to keep a door shut with something called *epoxy*, a substance he's never heard of in his life?

"I had to make do with what I had in my van," Urban says. "I mean, it's not like I was about to go back into Pork & Drones and get arrested again." He bends down and runs his finger along the crack between the closet door and the wall. "I don't see why it wouldn't work. If epoxy can seal a surfboard in the sun and salt water, it should be able to hold a closet shut."

Three quarters of the way up the closet, Urban begins squeezing the gray-white substance into the crack between the door and the wall.

Rex watches with a muted mixture of admiration and horror. Urban has always been a resourceful person, all those years living in his van have taught him to get the most out of almost anything, sand, surf, and insects included. He once told Rex that he needed less than 15 EuroDollars a month to survive. Rex wasn't sure how that was possible, but he believed him.

Urban finishes near the bottom of the door and then turns to Rex. "You have a hair dryer?"

"No."

"You have a couple billion EDs and don't have a hair dryer?"

"Sofina's bald and I towel dry. Not all of us have ponytails."

Urban runs his index finger along the epoxy in the door crack. "We have to find some way to dry it or else it could stay wet for days. We need a space heater or a blowtorch or something. Some way to apply heat."

They meet eyes.

"Is it still in the bathroom?" Urban asks.

"No. No way. Haven't we learned our lesson?"

"What choice do we have?"

"It's incriminating and Sofina's still here."

"Better hurry then."

Rex doesn't know why he's listening to Urban again, even as he hurries to the bathroom. And he knows he shouldn't be doing this, even as he removes the Taser from the top of the medicine cabinet. And he becomes certain that this is a terrible idea, even as he hands the Taser to Urban.

"Stand back," Urban says.

Urban tasers the closet door, zapping the epoxy every inch from the top to the bottom, and the room begins to smell like tomatoes and burnt marshmallows.

"Is that toxic?"

"Probably." Urban stands back to admire his work. He runs a finger over the tasered epoxy and smiles. "But it's working."

From the terrace, Rex hears the thudding of the delivery drone from the Paunchy Pilot restaurant, carrying the appetizers that Sofina had ordered earlier. He's glad to have an excuse to get away from the odor and goes outside where the drone has landed. He pulls from the refrigerated canister marked 'Knightly' a platter of cheese and crackers and a plate of deviled eggs.[18] When he returns to the room with the food, he almost pulls the sliding door shut but remembers the smell from the closet and leaves it open a crack. Inside, Sofina is staring hard at Urban, who holds the Taser in his hands like a guilty child.

"Urban, what are you doing with a Taser in my home?"

"Yeah, well, funny story, Sofina."

Rex bangs the appetizers on the coffee table. "The appetizers are here," he says and tosses half a deviled egg into his mouth. After two bites, he spits it back into his bare hand. "And they're horrible."

Sofina looks at Rex but is undeterred from her line of questioning. "Urban, again, why is there a Taser in my home?"

"We should send them back, get something that's edible." Rex says.

"Urban, I asked you a question."

"It's to dry the epoxy that I used to seal the closet door shut."

"Why do you have a *weapon* to begin with? That's what I want to know."

"I think I'm going to be sick," Rex says.

---

18 Approximate calorie count: 140 per egg

27

There's nowhere else Billy wants to be.

As he lies on the cozy hollow of Petty's stomach, with her cowgirl legs locked behind him, her café-au-lait nipples tilted sideways, and her blue hair bouncing on the side of her head like a cheering smurf, there's nowhere else he wants to be but inside her.

Not on Bougainville's ship.

Not in Kolkata.

Not in another body without an implanted biochip.

Let the cops arrest him. Let the prison officials strap him down and shove the mouth protector between his teeth. Let the minister pray, the warden issue the command, and the executioner pull the switch. Billy can now be exterminated, because he will have had this great cosmic moment. And in the greater cosmos, a great cosmic moment is all anyone can hope for. Her warm breath tickling his neck, the vise grip of her legs, her thin fingers in his ears. As he gently tastes the top of her scalp, he knows he loves her.

To think he'd been worried that he'd be unable to perform. It was all in his head, the problem being that his head was attached to his body. A body jam-packed with involuntary functions: breathing, digesting, blood pumping, hair growing, and who knows what else. He'd been afraid that he'd never feel the full satisfaction of his manhood again, and that the inability to reach this achievable Goal would lead to his death. But once she displayed her newly shaved marvelousness, with the light on the side table casting a shadow between her legs and forming a grand and glorious oval behind her. He knew he'd be fine. She'd be his retroactive first and last (possibly) and every woman in between.

She vacuums his left earlobe with her mouth and he's deafened by pleasant *smacking* sounds. She's obsessed with his ears, but there's no need to be self-conscious. He accepts her, and she accepts him, mutually trading on an 'as is' basis. No credits, no exceptions, no alterations, no returns. What love is. His big ears and her bowed legs. His prison sentence and her zombie fetish. He thrusts upward and finishes with an unexpected, electrifying wattage and a growl.

"No longer a virgin," she says, pulling away from his ear. "Not bad for your first time."

She tosses her head back and exposes a thin, flushed, vulnerable neck, that's red and raw where he'd been nibbling. She rocks forward, kisses him in his mouth, and then she leans over and turns off her eCatt on the table.

"Wait, did you just livestream us?"

"I livestream everything. I told you that."

"Will they know it's me?"

"Probably. *WeUs* has great facial recognition. I've never seen actually anybody who wasn't tagged, except for this guy from a lost tribe in the Amazon. He became famous for a while, and then he was tagged everywhere. But you've been away for a long time. Are you on any social media? Have a passport? Driver's license?"

"I'm in the California prisoner's database. If they see me, they'll come get me."

"We'll just have to figure out a way to prove your innocence then."

"My appeals have run out. That's why they were going to kill me. And I have a biochip inside me, so they can track me wherever I go. I was planning on running away to a slum in India to live, but now, with this, with you..."

"India's ice. I was watching this Bollywood vid once, where this zombie becomes a millionaire but can't find love because he's all cut up and bandaged and stuff. It was called *Karma Suture*. Have you seen it? The poor zombie can't even spend his money on anything good except to buy bodies at the morgue to eat. Oh, sorry. I didn't mean anything by that. I just..."

"It's okay."

"So yeah, then this zombie finds a smoking-hot untouchable zombie and they fall in Indian love, which is supposed to be the best kind because they have, like, ten thousand sexual positions. How is that even possible? But they don't kiss. Did you know zombies never kiss in Bollywood vids? Maybe I could get a job as an extra there. That'd be so ice."

She looks at her eCatt and almost elevates from the ground. "I'll be bitchin!" She points her eCatt so he can see their pornographic video playing. She's wriggling and bouncing and bucking beneath him, with a sly smile, as if she knows a special secret. His own body looks slightly paunchy in profile, but he's not too bad, all things considered. It's only his expression which, in contrast to hers, makes him look like he's trying to solve a math equation. He needs to work on that.

"What does that number mean?" he says, pointing at a counter in the lower right hand corner.

"That's the number of views. 235,000 already? OMFG!"

"How'd we get so many views? It just happened."

"It must be ... yeah, they've tagged you as the recently escaped serial killer and cannibal Billy the Goat. You're on all the feeds. We're viral. We're trending everywhere."

"Wait, what are you saying? Who knows it's me?"

"Anybody and everybody."

28

Bassia walks past the protesters on Columbus Ave, a leaderless cluster of the unemployed, uninsured, hungry, and homeless – with the usual scattering of opportunists, anarchists, and apocalyptians thrown in.

Like the Occupy Movements, the *gilets jaunes*, or 15-M Movement, these ongoing protests seem to lack coherence and direction. The protesters demand change, they *deserve* change, but precisely what that change should be, they don't seem to have any workable, overarching ideas. Nor does anyone else. All anyone knows is that sweeping changes have to happen, and soon. The status quo is untenable for the planet and its people.

Just past her, a throng of teenagers, mothers, and kids exit a grocery store with baskets and armfuls of stolen goods. As attorney general, it's her obligation to stop them. But these are good folks, most of them, in survival mode. And it's not like the governor and his cronies haven't effectively legalized banditry for themselves.

What is it they say?

The law is to justice what medicine is to immortality.

If only.

"Find me a sociopath to execute." That's what the governor had told her more than three months ago, when the

Supreme Court was getting ready to rule on *Penny-Miller v. Georgia* and end capital punishment. "A real sicko."

Abbot Swenson has long held presidential ambitions, and he might be close to realizing them with the notoriety he received from this reckless Last Days of Pompeii program, which was a disaster for California but not so bad for him. Is the country as a whole willing to give up the good fight for the planet and each other? That's what he intends to find out. The only other concern he has to address, coming from a progressive state, is to prove that he's tough on crime. And what could be more unimpeachable evidence of his toughness than being the last governor in the nation to execute a man? That single act would attest to his resolve.

Just as long as the man he executes has done things so horrible it'd be difficult for anyone to object.

As always, there's cruelty in expediency, but she performed her duty as she must and found the governor his man: a psycho with a nickname, the Goat, that she couldn't improve on if she tried. Though she had found him, she didn't actually want Billy Wharton to die and had always hoped that some last minute reprieve would be found. And it had in his escape.

The Fugitive Task Force has activated the biochip implanted behind the fourth rib on the Goat's right-hand side, but they're having difficulty getting a lock on his location. The biochips have been merely moderately successful since they were implemented. This information has been kept from the public, in order to maintain their usefulness as a deterrent, but that doesn't help in the event of an actual escape. So as of right now, they'll just have to wait for the Goat to pop up somewhere.

She looks at her eCatt, and there he is on video. It must be a joke. Some gifted high-school students, or media nerds at USC, or closet CGIers in the San Fernando Valley. Maybe some prankster animators and editors from Stanford. It can't be real, but it *looks* real. They're good, whoever they are. It's trending too.

Three hundred thousand views already and increasing fast.

Could it be real? Even a cannibal wouldn't be this stupid. *WeUs* has some of the best facial recognition available, and Billy Wharton must've known he'd be ID'd immediately. Yet here he is on her eCatt, naked, large-eared, with a painfully thin, half blue-haired woman wriggling ecstatically beneath him.

So he's not only escaped but stopped to have sex and upstream it for all who want to see. Can it really be him? If it is, it's a big F-U to those who'd tried to kill him, like the governor and by extension herself. If that's what he's after, he succeeded.

A large store window across the street explodes, and she flinches. The riot is behind her but as uncontained as the fires and floods. A huddle of people, many with hand-kerchiefs covering their noses and mouths, bound through the broken window, unconcerned with the jagged glass that lines the frame. She hurries on when she smells gas in the distance and a heavy pounding begins.

It must mean something that she's scurrying away while a wanted man is on her eCatt, having the time of his life. If he wasn't sociopathic, you'd have to hand it to him.

It's no joke. It's him. It's Wharton. There's no sense in denying it. There's a part of her, not the rational, prosecutorial side, but the miming, artistic side, the side that nobody knows, that thinks 'good for him.' If they catch him again, and they will, and they're still able to execute him, which they might be, then he can remember this last romp as he passes to the other side.

She ducks into a littered doorway set back from the street and takes a few deep breaths. A car races by and another store window smashes. There are cheers in the distance.

Her eCatt vibrates with the name: "John Missionary…John Missionary…John Missionary."

"Can you believe this guy?" he says like a bullfrog. He means Wharton. Missionary's a blowhard and a publicity seeker (who's rumored to have only one testicle), but he's undeniably good as Commander of the Fugitive Task Force. He's caught more than half a dozen escapees this year alone, and he won't let Bassia or anyone else forget it. "We've got information that he stole a pickup truck just outside the city and drove to the Pork & Drones Depot, where he bought marijuana, wine, condoms, and underwear. The store's facial and gait recognition got him."

"Underwear?"

"Yeah, the prisoners have been complaining about dirty underwear since TLC Corrections took over the business. There's a profit in unwashed underwear, I'm told. Dirty sheets too."

She knows all about it. In the back of the drawer of her desk is an offer for a seat on the board of TLC. If accepted, she could spend her days miming on the street, show up for the Board meeting at TLC every quarter, and still make as much money as she does now. She never liked TLC, nobody does, because with every sheet and pair of underwear that goes unchanged, with every overcrowded cell and dog-food dinner, they make more money. Yes, they're trying to leverage her position, gender, and reputation by bringing her on, but they're willing to pay her a substantial salary to do so. And there are days, long days, when the work she's doing is meaningless (at best) that she's tempted to accept the offer. Money or art? Justice or capitulation? Old questions raised anew. And all she knows is her own dissatisfaction and that of the rioters that surround her.

"I wish they'd privatize fugitive capture too," Missionary says. "I'd make a fortune."

"I'm supposed to meet the lieutenant governor tonight. I'll mention it to her."

"Will you?"

"No."

He sniffs disapprovingly and clears his throat. "You know I've caught more than half a dozen fugitives this year?"

"The number hasn't changed since you reminded me last week."

"It will today. The Goat did us a favor by stopping to bust a nut with Miss skinny blue hair. Of course, his biochip isn't working, but we fixed the Goat's location from the livestreaming account of the video and, unless he left, now have a position on him. A surveillance drone is on its way."

"You need anything more from me?"

"Yeah, privatize fugitive capture? Just kidding. Not really. But we're good. You can sit back, relax, and let the Missionary man handle it. I'll let you know when we've got him."

She's free of Billy Wharton for the time being. It's in Missionary's purview. Some small, conflicted part of her hopes that he kills Wharton. That'd be the best thing for all of them, Wharton included. That would save another fat file, another tiresome slag through the courts to make the legality of his execution retroactive to the day of his escape, which she's certain the governor will insist on, whether or not it's feasible. And it would give her another day to pursue the endless number of wrongful conviction cases on her desk, exonerate another innocent person unjustly imprisoned by the government she represents.

She steps out from the doorway and a kid runs past her carrying two six packs of beer and an armful of eCatts. "Get it while you can!" he yells, and she wonders if his opportunism has any degree of idealism – if he's seeking change or merely profit. Does he know that the current level of economic inequality is incompatible with liberal democracy? Is he trying to fix that in some small way? Is he going to drink the beer and sell the eCatts to get the courage and funds for another protest? She's not so naïve to believe that. He has needs of his own.

There is one last hope, the one that lies in the election recall papers in her briefcase, the ones she's delivering to Sofina. There is no time to waste. Bassia drops 40 EuroDollars in the cluttered shopping cart of an unconscious homeless man and hurries in the direction of Sofina's penthouse.

29

Half a million and counting.

That's how many people have watched Billy and Petty have sex on *WeUs* – even though they just did it. It boggles the mind. Don't people have anything better to do? Why aren't they having sex themselves instead of watching other people do it? It's like they don't know they're free. If you're just going to *watch*, you might as well be locked in a tuna can, like he was. Billy doesn't understand people anymore.

Petty has been watching the video over and over. She sidesaddles on his lap and shows him the comments:

Billy's killing it again!

bitch ain't heard of bareaway?
   #stupidhair #baldisbeautiful

Hope she doing that when he get electricuted!!!!!!

10 to 1 the goat eats her afterward
   #MeatIsMurder

He shouldn't get mad but can't help himself. They're reducing him to a killer and cannibal. Nobody seems to say anything nice about either of them, though people must've enjoyed the video to watch it and comment on it. Half a million people, that is.

A siren in the street.

He hears it faintly at first but it's getting louder. Are they coming for him? Is it for the fire or the floods? No, it must be him. They've locked in on his biochip or through the tag on the sex video or some other way. It doesn't matter. They're on their way, and his pleasant buzz has vanished: the wine, the pot, the post-sex bliss, all gone. He has only a few more minutes if he wants to get away. If he wants to live.

A sense of exhaustion overwhelms him. He's been on the run for just a few hours and already he's beat. This is why men give themselves up. It's the relentless tension, the heightened blood pressure, existing like an undiscovered hamster in a snake pit.

Petty hears the siren and knows what it means. "I'm sorry, Billy."

"It's not your fault. With this biochip in me, it's something I'll have to get used to until I can get it out. I just need to stay one step ahead of them somehow. Maybe I need a better disguise. I borrowed a woman's clothes earlier but—"

Her eyes light up. "Come with me."

In the bathroom, he sits on the toilet with his head bent back over the sink. He's naked from the waist up and there's a towel around his neck. Petty massages his scalp with her wet fingers and almost suffocates him by playfully rubbing her breasts into his face. She snaps on a couple of latex gloves and grabs the bottle of blue dye from the edge of the bathtub. He closes his eyes as she rubs the dye into his hair. As his head tingles and burns, he imagines a life with Petty. A small cottage on the Oregon coast, chickens in the yard, ganja in the garden, and nothing but wet forest for miles. A long way from Kolkata, but so what? He'll take his meds, drink, smoke, meditate, and make love to Petty every morning and night.

Her delicate fingers slide back and forth on his scalp, and he could go to sleep if the State of California wasn't trying to recapture and kill him.

"I've got an idea." Petty steps back to admire her work. "I'll get us our own *WeUs* channel, and we can livestream everything we do, eat, sleep, talk, shower, shave, have sex, everything. And you can explain yourself, tell everyone how you didn't really kill or eat all those people or, at least, didn't mean to."

"If we do that, you could end up in prison yourself. Because you can't know I'm an escaped convict. I have to be just Billy to you, a guy you met at the store and liked. Remember that. If anyone asks, you don't know who I am. Find a story and stick with it. No matter what."

"I'm good at stories."

"One more thing…I know we've only known each other a short time, but you're the most beautiful woman I've seen in a decade. The sexiest too. And the nicest. And the coolest. And most interesting. And fun."

"Glad you noticed."

"I'd like to ask you, if I'm recaptured, and they don't kill me right away, if we could still see each other and have conjugal visits. Thing is, we'd have to do something else first. Know what I mean?"

She walks around the chair and kneels so she's looking him in the eye. Her large, lagoon-like eyes blink a couple of times and, for once, she seems at a loss for words. "Are you—?" is all that she can manage.

A droplet emerges from the pool of her left eye, and it's as if God had saved him for this moment, let him escape and put off his execution so he could be here. He realizes that she's on her knees, not him, and that he should be. He falls to his knees in front of her.

"You'd make me the happiest man on earth if you'd marry me, Petty?"

"OMFG, that's so ice, like, a big, fat frozen icicle."

"Will you?"

"Oh yeah, like, I will, yes ... I do. I do too." She takes his hands. "Let's make a run for it. Move to India like you want or to Bolivia like the outlaws in an ancient vid I saw once: *David Cassidy and the Sundance Kid* I think it was called. We can livestream our adventures for money and just go ..."

"We will but—" The siren is close, too close. In the other room, red and blue lights flash through the window. "There's just one more thing I have to do. I don't want to die, and I need an insurance policy in case they catch me again. And I think I know how I can get one. I thought of it while you were doing my hair. I just need to take care of one small thing and then we can run away together. All I need is an address."

30

Sofina realizes that she's the only sane person in her penthouse.

Which is an exceptionally low bar, it being only Rex, Urban, and her. She looks at the closet with the hardened epoxy between the door and frame. The sex animate is still inside. But did either Rex or Urban consider how the door would ever open again? What if someone needs a jacket or umbrella? They'll have to open it some time.

She regards them now, standing rigid on opposite sides of her like two naughty schoolchildren. Rex with a half-eaten deviled egg in his hand, and Urban trying to hide a Taser behind his back, as if she'll forget about it. She only wishes she could. He hasn't answered her question about why he has a weapon to begin with, but she doesn't care anymore.

She needs to focus on the bigger picture, use her half-alien brain for the broader perspective.

"Your father wasn't really an alien."

Those were some of the last words her mother ever spoke. Sofina'd returned from college and was sitting by her mother's bed. Her mother had lost her hair, and Sofina was looking at the indentation on the left side of her head. The same indentation that she'd later discover in her own. She'd wanted to come home earlier, but her mother had insisted she stay to finish her exams. "They aren't giving you that scholarship to visit me," her mother told her.

"I know Dad wasn't an alien, Mom." Sofina stroked her mother's head. "I stopped believing that around the time I stopped believing in Santa Claus."

Her mother smiled sadly. "I just…I wanted you to think so. When you were younger, I didn't want you to feel that you were missing something because he went away. I wanted to make it seem special somehow. He liked his drugs, booze, and women too much to stay. An old story. He didn't know babies."

"It's okay, Mom."

Her mother's voice was getting weaker, her breaths shallower. She spoke slowly, carefully. "I didn't want you to ever think it was your fault, because it wasn't. Some people don't know how to love. I tried to make up for it but…I don't know."

"Your love is all I need. More than enough."

Her mother shifted her hand, as if waving away the praise. "But you *are* very special, Sofi. You are. You *do* have special powers, I can see it. In you. Not because I'm your mother. I believe that you *do* have a secret mission. We just don't know what it is yet. But you're close to finding out. So close."

There's a knock on the front door. She blinks away all thoughts of her mother and re-engages with the tasks at hand. She turns to Urban who's still holding the Taser behind his back. "Get rid of that thing. There's a garbage shoot in the hallway and that's going down it ASAP."

As she heads to the door, she looks out past the terrace through the smoky and smoggy San Francisco sky. She can't see the building across the street. And somewhere, just a few blocks away, there is a riot and slightly further on a mutinous ocean and, a few miles in the other direction, a fire uncontained. There's nothing in California, no person, place, or thing that isn't crying out. The current governor is worse than useless, and Sofina has a gifted and formidable ally in Bassia Augustine. Her mission has never been clearer or more important.

She turns back to Rex and Urban. "What happens next in this room will determine not just my future, but the future of the entire state. Both of you better understand that."

She opens the front door to reveal the attorney general.

31

Petty shows Billy the map on her eCatt.

"It's not far at all," she says. "It's a building for rich people. Are you sure we can't just make a run for it to India or Bolivia?"

"It's this biochip. I'm not sure what the range is or how long they work, but I need to make sure they won't execute me if I'm recaptured. I want to live more than ever, so we can be together."

"I'll never let you die, Billy."

The siren has gone silent, and the police drone hovering outside the window shines a bright spotlight into the room. Billy pulls Petty to the floor behind the loveseat.

"What about a presidential pardon?" Petty says. "I saw a vid once where the wife of a Wall Street banker got her husband pardoned because she knew the president was a zombie. He got bitten right after he was elected, but they hid it really well and nobody knew except this one woman. It was called *ZombieGate*. Have you seen it?"

Billy shakes his head. "I don't think the president cares about me."

"But we're famous! That's something. Maybe I could go on a *WeUs – > Talk* and tell everyone how sweet you are, and that you really don't know if you killed those people, so it's unfair that they want to kill you."

It's not a bad idea, Billy thinks, only that her credibility might be destroyed by the pornographic video they just made. Does pornography destroy credibility anymore? Did it ever? Celebrities were making lots of sex videos when he was locked up. But his case seems to be different. "I don't think I'd get much sympathy. Did you see all those comments? They're wondering if I'm going to eat you."

An unmodulated voice comes from the drone outside the window: "William Wharton, leave any weapons in plain sight and come out with your hands up."

He lifts his head slightly and sees the drone hovering like a giant, predatory hummingbird, slowly rotating a spotlight around the room. He ducks before the light reaches him. He waits for the light to pass and then grabs the Glock from the table.

"I have to get out of here," he says.

"Okay, give me a moment. I've seen this in a vid before." She glances to the kitchen on the other side of the room. "The kitchen window is only six feet above the ground. If we can make it there, you might be able to run away." She looks at him. "You've got blue hair now and the drone will be trying to track you from above, so if you keep your head down, they might not know it's you."

"What about the biochip?"

"You'll have to take your chances with that. But this might buy you some time."

They time the rotating spotlight and crawl side by side on their stomachs around the coffee table and into the kitchen, where they are blocked from the drone's view by a counter. The kitchen window behind them is in full view. It's five feet from the floor and behind the sink.

The unmodulated voice speaks again: "William Wharton, come out with your hands up. Now."

"The next time, after the light comes around, out you go," she says. "You remember where you're going?"

He nods. "This has been the best day of my life."

"I love you, Billy. Now don't get caught and come back to me. Here comes the light, okay wait, wait and…go now!"

He climbs over the sink and slides out of the window feet first, almost banging his head on the upper sill. He falls fast and hard. Did she push him? The ground arrives. He crumbles on the cement and winds up on his side amidst some trash and dog poop. He looks up at the window. Is that her idea of six feet? He checks the alley, feels for the Glock, and then starts running, an armed, blue-haired man determined to save his life and intended marriage.

32

"Bassia, thanks for getting here so quickly."

Sofina smiles warmly and leads the attorney general into the penthouse. As Bassia crosses the threshold of the door, Urban, who's been camped against the front wall, deftly slips into the hall with the Taser behind his back. Thankfully, Bassia doesn't seem to notice or care.

"We knew this day was coming," Bassia says. "With the fires, floods, and the recent earthquake warnings, we've hit the climate trifecta. Fortunately, they've located the serial killer Billy the Goat. That's one thing going our way. They haven't picked him up yet, but it should only be a matter of time."

"Billy the Goat? Wasn't he due to be executed tonight?" Rex asks.

He's sidled between Bassia and Sofina, who almost asks him to leave, but reconsiders. Whatever keeps him within the boundaries of normal, civilized behavior is good enough for now. At least he got rid of that half-eaten deviled egg he'd been walking around with.

"That's him," Bassia says. "He escaped out during transit to the execution chamber. I never trusted those self-driving vans, even though he was traveling with live guards as well. The Fugitive Task Force is looking for him now."

"Can he still be executed?' Urban has reappeared in the doorway. His hands are empty, so he's gotten rid of the Taser. At least he can follow instructions. Now he needs to make himself scarce. And if he won't, she will.

Bassia turns to him. "And you are?"

"That's Urban," Sofina says. "Who's just leaving." She waits for Urban to move away and points her chin at the briefcase in Bassia's hand. "I see you have the papers."

"Awaiting your signature."

Sofina leads Bassia to the coffee table where the appetizers are laid out in front of them.

"I hope you don't mind me mentioning, Sofina" Bassia says. "But there's a strange odor in here. Faint, but I've smelled it before. It's sort of sickly sweet, like burning or decomposing—"

"That'd be the deviled eggs from the Paunchy Pilot," Rex says. He's followed them to the couch. "They always taste like dead people."

"You know what dead people taste like?" Bassia asks, perplexed.

"I, uh, tried them earlier."

"The eggs or a dead person?"

Sofina's had enough. She hands the appetizers to Rex. "Take these dead-smelling eggs and yourself away."

Sofina sniffs and realizes that there is indeed a strange odor in the room, a certain sourness smokiness that's more than deviled eggs. She hopes it has nothing to do with the sex animate in the closet.

When Rex departs, she says, "It's you and me, Bassia. There's not a single other politician or official I trust."

"The reason I ran for attorney general was to right injustices. That's all. I thought I could do my part, case by case, person by person. But now I see that the injustice is on a far greater scale. The environment affects every one of us, and if men like Abbot Swenson, who's been missing for hours, aren't stopped, there'll be no justice for anyone."

Bassia opens her briefcase on her knees and sorts through the election recall documents.

"Any idea who kidnapped the governor?" It's Urban, from nowhere, and Sofina's just about to tell him to get away when Bassia wheels on him.

"Who said he was kidnapped?"

"Uh, you did." He tugs on the heavy ponytail hanging on his shoulder.

"I said he's *missing*. You said *kidnapped*."

"Yeah, no, I just assumed, I mean … didn't you assume he was kidnapped?"

"I did." Rex has deposited the deviled eggs elsewhere and circled back.

Sofina's had enough. "Rex and Urban go away. Now."

Bassia hands a pen to Sofina and points at a line on the bottom of the document.

"Sign and date," Bassia says, "and there's no turning back."

Sofina takes a deep breath. "So we're clear … here's the plan. One, we recall the governor's election. Two, I run for governor in the subsequent election, and back your campaign for lieutenant governor. Three, together we fight like hell to save our state and the people in it. Four, after I complete a single term as governor, I support your own candidacy for governor, and we keep fighting the good fight. Agreed?"

Bassia nods and Sofina is about to sign the paper when there are three rapid knocks on the front door.

33

After the three knocks comes a heavy, impatient hammering.

Bang, bang, bang, bang.

The penthouse goes still. There's no movement and no other sound, as if the banging is a judge's gavel or a mute button, as if they all know something momentous is about to happen. But what? Rex feels each blow on the door in his chest, knees, and forehead. Who the hell can it be? Has Sofina invited someone else? A friendly neighbor? A colleague? Everyone is here who's supposed to be here.

The police. It must be the police. They've discovered that he and Urban killed the governor, and they've come to arrest them. To pry open the epoxied closet, expose the governor's body, and drag them away in handcuffs.

Bang, bang, bang, bang.

How did they find out so fast? Because everything is recorded these days, that's how. Cameras are omnipresent. Drones are ubiquitous. Eyes and ears are everywhere and nothing is private. Someone witnessed the kidnapping of the governor in the street. Or saw them ride up in the elevator. Or spied them through the window as they shoved the body in the closet. Who knows? There's a hundred ways. It's over. They're doomed. They need an explanation.

The governor asked for it?

The governor hid in the closet to spy on Sofina and sat on a Taser?

The Taser was mis-calibrated and delivered a virtual lighting strike?

Sofina walks toward the door with a studious expression on her face. She's probably thinking that it's the governor knocking, and she needs to excuse why all these people, including the attorney general, are in her home.

Rex turns to Urban, who merely shrugs as if he doesn't care. How does he do it? Is it the ponytail? Or has all the surfing numbed all his senses? Which means Rex will have to bear the psychological burden of their misdeeds alone? He suppresses an urge to sprint onto the terrace and leap. At least, that'd be quick and, after the initial trauma, painless.

Bang, bang, bang, bang.

He has a few final seconds to be considered the good man he was meant to be: innocent, poetic, loyal, and generally 'well liked' in a majority of student surveys. When the door opens, he'll be a murderer, an assassin. He already is, but nobody knows that, which makes all the difference at this point.

In these, his last moments as a free and seemingly decent man, he ponders the difference between a murderer and an assassin. All assassins are murderers, true, but is every murderer an assassin? A good riddle, like the one James Joyce posed, wondering if it was possible to cross Dublin without passing a pub. Of course, that's easy if you stop in every one. Joyce should've known that. So there must be an answer there to the murderer vs. assassin riddle as well. You're not an assassin if you kill everybody?

Bang, bang, bang, bang.

Sofina barely opens the door and it swings wide on the hinges, cracking the back wall and rebounding back with such force that it closes again. There's a man outside but the door closed so quickly it was hard to tell who it was. He didn't look like a policeman though.

Sofina opens the door again, and a blue-haired man with a gun steps into the penthouse. Rex jumps. Sofina falls back. Urban groans. Bassia doesn't move.

"Quiet down!" the blue-haired man screams though no one is talking. And then, more quietly, "Why are there so many people here?"

"It's the Goat!" the attorney general says.

"I wasn't expecting so many people."

"I ran into him earlier," Urban says. "He's changed his hair color."

"Quiet down! Go over there with your hands in the air."

"Where?"

"I don't know. There's too many of you. Somewhere against the wall. Over there." He wags his gun carelessly.

They walk toward the wall as ordered, all except for Sofina, who has remained beside the front door, not three feet from the armed man. With a spastic flick of his hand, Rex signals for her to run through the open door and escape. If nothing else, it'd force the blue-haired man – Billy the Goat? – to make a decision. But Rex can't get Sofina's attention. She stares at the man with unblinking eyes and looks like she's not breathing. She isn't panicked and doesn't seem eager to leave. Quite the opposite. Can she be that skilled a compartmentalizer?

It's not until Rex is lined up against the wall with the others that Sofina finally speaks.

"Billy, is that you?"

She knows him? Is she joking? Did she have something to do with his trial? Or visit him in prison? Was he a former employee at Share4All? Rex can't wrap his mind around it.

"It is you," she says.

Why is she being so nice?

"Hi, Sofi."

Sofi? He calls her *Sofi*? Rex doesn't even call her Sofi. Why such familiarity with his wife, the lieutenant governor? He should address her as 'Your honor,' or at least 'Mrs. Nightly.' He's a convict, who should be dead, and he's calling his wife by a *pet* name. Who does he think he is with his blue hair and ears like a human mouse?

"That's Mrs. Sofina Nightly to you!" Rex says, but he hears how stupid it is as he says it. This guy has a gun, and he's standing on formality.

"It's okay, Rex. It's Billy Wharton. We went to the senior prom together."

His mind is a sinkhole, thoughts collapsing in on one another. So wait, it wasn't the police knocking at the door coming to arrest him; it was Billy the Goat, the man that he and Urban had tried to save earlier this afternoon and, apparently, somehow did. Is he hallucinating? Sofina went to the prom with a guy named Billy, a quiet cross-country runner with big ears who was her first kiss, her first boyfriend, her first–

He can no longer contain himself.

"Wait, so, you mean…*him*? This guy? Billy the *Goat* was your first?" He feels like he inhaled a fish bone. "He takes your virginity in the back of a PT Cruiser and then goes on to kill nine people?"

"Allegedly," Billy says and smiles proudly, waving his gun like a child's toy.

The Wall Street Journal CEO Interview: Sofina Nightly Share4All, Inc.

January 23, 2026

How does it feel to be one of the world's newest billionaires?
It doesn't feel like anything at all. Not yet. Our lifestyle hasn't changed. All that's changed is my husband and I have started looking for a penthouse in San Francisco, and I get a lot more calls from charities and alma maters. I never had much to begin with, so other than that, it's just a lot of zeroes. I'm not sure what to do with it all yet, but I assure you I'll find something.

You've been described as a diligent visionary. Does the definition fit?
I'll take that. Though I don't think a vision is ever fully realized. No goal is ever reached, but it focuses the work and

that's what truly matters. The important stuff, the discoveries and the breakthroughs, are found in the day-to-day efforts. It's a process. It requires faith, belief in yourself.

There are rumors that you were forced out as CEO of Share4All. Is that true?
Not at all. I went willingly. I've done all I can at Share4All. It's time for someone else to take the helm, someone with experience running a larger company. I want to spend more time with my husband after working fifteen hour days, seven days a week. I'm ready to move on to other challenges.

Share4All was revolutionary not so much in the concept of sharing goods but in scale and scope, in the idea that almost everything can be shared. Critics have complained that it was anti-jobs and anti-growth because the more goods that are shared, the less that need to be produced. How do you respond?
Share4All isn't anti anything. Its mission was to make sharing easy, to make most efficient use of the goods that are already available. Any increase in efficiency, which can be defined as doing more with less, is disruptive, and that disruption has both good and bad consequences. I will tell you that Share4All has been a positive for the environment, mankind's greatest threat, because of the reduction in manufacturing, transportation, and waste and the attendant reductions in carbon emissions, toxic effluence, and pollution.

Tell us about your first shareholder Benny, the initial inspiration for Share4All, when you saw him sliding down a mountain of trash in a bathtub. He went from homeless to multimillionaire. What is he doing now?

Benny lives on top of the landfill where I first saw him, only now in two large shipping containers with plumbing, a bar, an entertainment center, and a massive hot tub. He bought containers for all his friends as well. He says he doesn't want to go anywhere, ever. He's happy as a clam right where he is.

Have you been to visit him?

Not yet. My husband Rex has been there a number of times and says it's wonderful. They drink and smoke more than they should, but so does my husband. He told me he wouldn't mind moving there.

Abbott Swenson, in his campaign for governor, is getting an awful lot of traction with his so-called Last Days of Pompeii program, which concedes that there's nothing that can be done for our planet and by extension ourselves, so why bother trying. Any thoughts?

That program is cynical, negligent, and catastrophic.

Last question. There've been reports that you're considering a run for lieutenant governor of California in opposition to Mr. Swenson.

That's not a question.

Are you?
I haven't made any commitments yet, but if I believed I'd be able to make a contribution in that space, I'd consider it.

Is that a yes?
It's not a no.

Thank you for your time.

Sofina Nightly is the Founder and former President and CEO of Share4All, Inc., which as of this date, January 23, 2026, has a market capitalization exceeding 27 billion EDs.

PART III

4:44 PM – 7:48 PM
June 16, 2029

34

"Why lock us in the bathroom?"

The bathroom is crowded with the three of them: Rex, Urban, and Bassia. It reminds Urban of the last time he rode the subway in New York City – only with a claw foot bathtub, travertine sink, and toilet along for the ride. Predictably, Rex has positioned himself next to the medicine cabinet, and Urban can only hope he won't indulge himself further.

"He locked us in here so he could be alone with your wife ... his ex-girlfriend," Bassia says.

She's a very pretty woman, but in a quiet way that you don't notice until you're next to her. Her eyes are large and expressive, taking in everything around her with a perfect mix of bemusement and concern. Has he seen her before? Maybe on the news. Why is he so nervous? Is it because she's so powerful? Or pretty? Or both?

"I haven't been without my eCatt unless I was surfing in five or six years," Urban says. "I feel naked," he adds stupidly.

"Do you surf naked?" she asks with a thin smile.

"Only when I need a longer fin." He chances an old joke, and she laughs, just once. But once is enough.

Rex opens the medicine cabinet and looks inside. He fingers the bottles carefully, like an archeologist, and then pulls out a bottle of GLIDERALL[19]. He opens the cap and shakes out a single red-orange pill.

"I wouldn't," Urban says.

"At this point, why not?"

"We need to keep our heads."

Rex replaces the bottle but keeps the pill in his hand.

"He's right," Bassia says. "Does anyone have any way to communicate with the outside world?"

She doesn't get an answer, because they all already know.

The Goat made them toss their eCatts onto the coffee table before they entered the bathroom, and he also had the foresight to hit the 1999 Privacy switch so no other device could listen to him inside the penthouse.

"Believe it or not, I ran into him earlier," Urban says. "Outside the Pork & Drones Depot. We literally smacked into each other."

"You sure it was him?" Bassia asks.

"He didn't have blue hair then, but yeah. I'd recognize those massive ears anywhere."

"What was he doing at Pork & Drones? What did he buy? The more we know the better."

"I don't know. I was leaving very quickly. He was on his way in."

Urban stares at Bassia for a long moment. It's her eyes. They're unforgettable. "I've seen you before too," he says.

"You think you've seen everyone before."

---

19 Side effects of GLIDERALL include severe abdominal pain, spastic colon, hernias, hemorrhoids, anal fissures as well as instant death.

"Yeah, but you were doing this mime stuff at Fisherman's Wharf. Your face was covered up except for your eyes, and you did this sad pantomime that I think was about being lost and alone. It was really good though, in a sad way. That was you, wasn't it? It must've been you."

"There used to be a lot of mimes at the Wharf," she says and turns away – too quickly it seems. "Let's focus on more important things. We know three things about the Goat. One, he was at Pork & Drones Depot. Two, he had sex with a strange woman on *WeUs* just before he got here."

"Wait, he had sex *already*?" Rex says. "With another woman? The guy's unstoppable."

"Three, he went to the prom with Sofina where, I guess, he took her virginity." She turns to Rex, who stares at his feet.

"I wonder if you have any surfing skills that might help us," Bassia says to Urban. "I'm just reaching for something, anything that might help us."

"I can paddle for a long time and pop up very quickly," Urban says. He clears a space on the bathroom floor, then lies down, pulls his ponytail behind his back, and then pops to his feet and extends his hands as if he's on a board.

"Huh," Bassia says. "Not as helpful as I'd hoped."

What was he thinking? She's turning him into an idiot. It's her eyes. They're so warm and alive. He could swim in her eyes, perhaps even surf.

"I'm sorry, I just– I mean, that was ..."

"Impressive, in its way. Not helpful, but impressive." She laughs once. "Were you always a surfer?"

"I used to be a lawyer, believe it or not." He wonders if she might've heard of him, if they ever crossed paths back in the day. "I worked death penalty cases until I started surfing full time about fifteen years ago."

"Why'd you quit the law?"

"I guess I burned out. It just got to me. I mean, maybe this isn't something I should say to the attorney general, but it was the injustice, the randomness of it all that got to me. At some point, I just couldn't do it anymore. I don't know if you understand."

"I do. Maybe more than you think."

She looks at him more closely and touches him lightly on the back of his hand. When she pulls away a second later, he can still feel her there. And he can still feel her as she explores the bathroom walls and ceilings, checking for cracks or faults. And as she tests the toilet lid and steps into the bathtub to study the shower nozzle.

A hollow pop from outside the door echoes within the bathroom walls. Rex reflexively swallows the pill in his hand, and Urban turns to Bassia.

"That was a gunshot," she says.

35

1.2 million views and counting.

Petty sits on the loveseat watching her own vid go full avalanche on *WeUs*. It has a warning about 'inappropriate content' and an age gateway, but that's not stopping anybody. She and Billy are becoming more famous every second with sub-vids, comments, and hashtags, and they're getting snapped, tweeted, spiN/Spun, and ping*ponged all over the place. It's strange; she should feel better. *WeUs* has activated ads so she's making money, making thousands of friends and fans, and yet she's all alone in her small apartment as the world watches her have sex with a condemned man, a man who's gone away to beg the lieutenant governor not to kill him.

Some of the feeds are now saying that Billy dated this woman in high school. Some even have pictures of Billy and her at the senior prom, but who knows if it's real? It's Billy all right in the pics; she can tell by his goofy smile and ears. He looks so young and cute. She wishes she knew him then. She'll take their word for it that it's Sofina Nightly with him. But were they ever together, or did someone just mash up the images? It's impossible to tell anymore. They're saying that this Sofina's, like, really, really rich and that she started that Share4All thing, which Petty has used herself. Does Billy want to get back together with her for her money? Impossible. Petty knows who Billy loves and it's not some rich, political bitch.

She's never using Share4All again, no matter what. And what's a *lieutenant* governor do anyway? Govern the lieutenants? How stupid is that?

She returns to the vid of herself and admires the snappy bouncing of her side boob beneath him, which looks pretty sexy, even if she does think so herself. There's a bottle-cap–sized bruise on her thigh that she's never noticed before. How did that happen? It's as if she's watching someone else, a sexy, bruised, side-boobed woman; she likes the way she grinds and grabs his ears like the reins of a horse. She feels the desire all over again, and it feels like living, really and truly living. Billy, Billy, Billy.

1.3 million views.

She can still feel him inside her, still hear his thick panting, and smell the sweet vanilla of his head. She'd trade a million of those views if she could be sure that he'd come back to her.

Was it in *TriBite VII: Musky in Minneapolis* where Emily and Gerald were separated by undeath when one of them was bitten? And when Emily realized she couldn't save the zombified Gerald, she became a zombie herself rather than live without him. It's the same with Billy and her. It's all super quick, but who's to judge? Who's to judge what's really living?

If they're going to lock him up forever, she'll move into his cell. If they're going to execute him, she'll hold his hand and die with him. And livestream it. How ice would that be? And then they could be buried together in one of those unmarked graves, which would later be discovered by stoned teenagers who'd visit them at midnight on the date of their execution for a thousand years as if they were musicians.

1.35 million views.

She needs her own channel on *WeUs* and to start selling Billy & Petty merchandise. The cannibal and the cutie. No, she can't label him like that. It's better not to do that at all. Better to keep it pure and don't sell out like artists used to do a hundred years ago. Why didn't they? Did they not need the money? Or was it for love? Did they love their art the way she loves Billy and didn't want anything to spoil it?

Her heart sinks at the thought of his recapture. She needs to find him, to help him. Why did she ever let him go? Why didn't she follow him?

She pulls up the address of Sofina Nightly in her eCatt. That's where Billy is, and that's where she needs to be. It's not far, just a few minutes away. But she's famous now; she'll be recognized. She goes into her bedroom, puts on a pair of 1980s–style wayfarer sunglasses, plops a vintage fedora over her half-blue half-bare head, and darts out the door.

36

Billy stares at the bullet hole, a round, black void in the hardwood floor.

A few moments ago, he'd been hugging Sofi and holding the pistol behind her back when it fired. In prison, he'd been told that Glocks have a hair-trigger, and two cons limped on poorly half-reconstructed knees to prove it. (TLC Corrections refused to pay for comprehensive knee replacements). But he never thought the gun would be *that* sensitive.

Fortunately, the bullet missed Sofi's legs and ass. And there were no screams from anyone on the floor below, so it's no harm, no foul as far as Billy's concerned. But Sofi doesn't seem to feel that way. She seems scared and confused. He's apologized a few times, and she eventually accepted it in a way that reminded him why he used to love her. She's forgiving, Sofi is, and that's good thing.

There's pounding on the bathroom door, and someone like Sofi's husband is yelling, "Sofina? Are you okay? Sofina? Sofina?"

"I'm fine," she calls.

"Did he hurt you? Is he hurting you?" Her husband again, sounding like a world-class whiner.

186

"Quiet down!" Billy says. "She said she's fine, so quiet down!"

He hopes that Sofi knows that he's not really like this: holding people hostage, shooting into the floor, and saying 'quiet down' all the time like his third-grade English teacher. He's overstimulated and maybe still a little high. And there's too many unexpected people here, too much going on.

Sofi circles the bullet hole, and then settles on the couch. She seems unhappy. This is not the way he wanted this to go.

"I'm sorry, Sofi. Don't be nervous."

He sits a few feet away from her on the couch and lays the touchy Glock on its side between them. He stares at her profile. Her lower lip is quivering, and she's older than he'd been imagining in his cell, with a thin web of wrinkles around her eyes. She smells like a bakery, bread and muffins. He wants to reach out and touch her, but his hands are shaking. He tries for something nice to say.

"You look good bald, Sofi."

"Nobody calls me Sofi anymore."

"I'll stop if you like."

"You can call me Sofi, Billy."

She smiles sadly and, somewhere in her eyes, he spies the girl she used to be: the unselfish, pass-first point guard on the basketball team, student body vice president, and valedictorian, who made her own clothes because she couldn't afford to buy them. He never understood why she went out with him, for whom high school was an upheaval of hair, hormones, and three mile races, but she did. Somehow, she did.

"Billy, you have to let them go. Then you have to turn yourself in. That's it. That's how this has to end."

"They want to kill me."

He puts his hands under his thighs to stop them from shaking. The Glock is as close to her as it is to him, and with his hands beneath his legs, she could easily grab it. If she wants to shoot him, let her shoot him. He'd prefer to die like that than strapped to an electrified chair. But if he remembers correctly, Sofi always hated guns.

"That's the first time I've ever fired a gun, believe it or not. I don't want to hurt anybody, Sofi. I know I'm supposed to be this serial killer and cannibal ... but I'm just a regular, nice guy. You remember, don't you?"

"Billy, I ..."

"Can't we just talk for a moment, Sofi? Please? I've been locked in a tuna can for ten years but I followed your career. I knew when you got married to that guy ..." He cocks his head toward the bathroom door. "I saw when you started that company and made all that money. What's that like? To be so rich?"

"Ah, Billy. I don't know. It takes away some stress from some places and adds it in others."

"You didn't have any money when we went out. You were the poorest person I knew back then, only nobody else knew it. Somehow nobody else ever knew."

"I made up for it in other ways, but Billy ..."

"And I saw when you became the lieutenant governor too. I would've voted for you if I could've, but I was on death row and all. I don't know why you never visited or called. Were you embarrassed about me?"

"No, of course not. I've just been so busy all these years. I ignored everything but what I was doing. I didn't know

Billy the Goat was *you*, and all anyone ever called you was the Goat. Even when they chose you for execution, they just called you the Goat. It never crossed my mind that you could be you."

"You didn't hear about it from someone back in high school?"

"We didn't have that many friends in high school, Billy, either of us. Remember? The ones we had have scattered and a PR person handles all my social media, so ... And you were Billy Wharton back then."

"I still am. I still *am* Billy Wharton. I love you, Sofi." Did he just say that? What about Petty? He swallows hard. "I mean, I lov*ed* you and it's sort of still there, but not like, alive anymore. Does that make sense?"

"It does, Billy. I loved you too and still do in some way, I suppose. That's why you have to turn yourself in. I can help you. Let me take care of it."

"Do you ever think of that first night? In the back of that old PT Cruiser. Remember ..."

"Billy, no, this is too much."

"Because I've thought about it. A lot. And I mean a *lot*. I spent years staring at the walls of my cell, meditating and going over every second of my life. One month, I tried to reimagine everything in my life from my first memory as a baby up until that moment in the cell. One of the things I lingered on was us, the parties, the prom, the beers, the 7-Eleven. Thank heaven for 7-Eleven, huh?"

She almost laughs. Or did she just swallow? "Billy, this isn't right."

"Maybe not, but I guess that's what I'm here for. To remind you that I'm human, not a *goat*."

"I know that, but did you really kill all those people?"

"I don't know. I was off my medications and blacked out."

"But you're on them now, right? Your medications?"

"I didn't bring them to the execution chamber with me, if that's what you're asking. I asked, but they told me that there aren't any mental illnesses in the ground, only grave ones. They thought that was funny."

She shakes her head. "Maybe you're at risk now, though, without your medication. Maybe you'll start– Oh God, you have to go, Billy. At least that. At least go."

"The pills I took yesterday should be in my system for a while, so it's not like I'm gonna eat one of those people in the bathroom. I'm not even hungry." He laughs, but she doesn't. "Sorry. Bad joke. Just trying to ease the tension." He shifts on the couch and watches the Glock rock back and forth before settling. "I'm a vegetarian now, Sofi, even the idea of meat makes me sick. Look, I'm sorry about all that, I just… This has been a crazy day with me escaping execution and then meeting a woman and getting engaged."

"Wait, since your escape?"

"Yeah, I just asked a woman to marry me. It's amazing how fast things happen in the outside world these days. We had sex too. You can watch it on your eCatt, if you want."

"You filmed yourself having sex?"

"She did and then she agreed to marry me. Or vice versa. I'm not sure which happened first."

"That's great, Billy, congratulations… but this is a bad situation."

"You know, since I've escaped I've met the *nicest* people. In prison, everybody's so uptight and violent all the time. It's hard to make friends. On the outside it seems like every-body's gotten nicer and crazier and the men lend other men their sex dolls and women want to have sex all the time and … all sorts of good stuff."

"Billy, why come here?"

He glances at the closed bathroom door. It's unignorably quiet in there. He wonders if they're planning to escape.

"I just want to ask you … to make sure … that if the police catch me again … if you could stop them from executing me? I know you're only the lieutenant governor, but please, Sofi. I don't want to die like that. So will you? Will you promise me?"

37

They're going to kill him.

That's what Petty thinks when she arrives out-side Sofina Nightly's condominium building and sees the drones, the police cars, the black Fugitive Task Force van, and a dozen or more heavily armed men and women. She can tell it's a building for the .01%, by the marble foyer inside and the safari animal sculptures outside, so it must be the right place.

She walks toward the yellow tape which reads:

POLICE LINE – DO NOT CROSS – POLICE LINE – DO NOT CROSS

She has to stop them from killing Billy, even if it means sac-rificing her own life. A number of cops seem to be looking up, and she does the same. A set of balconies rise into the sky like a giant step ladder before disappearing into the smoke. Nobody can even see the top of the building, so what're they all looking at? Shouldn't these cops be doing something more useful like saving the city from the fires or floods, rather than staring at empty balconies and trying to kill Billy?

What can she possibly do against all these armed cops? She's spent too much of her time watching vids, when she should have been practicing karate or learning SWAT techniques. She has no idea how to help anyone escape from anything except slow-moving zombies and, sometimes, the beady eyes of the boss at the Porker.

In every vid she's ever seen, everybody has a plan, even the zombies. The plan never works out the way anyone wants it to, but it always works out in some way. So she comes up with one: she'll duck under the police tape, then sneak into the building, and climb to the top floor where Sofina Nightly's penthouse is located. Okay, all good, but then ... then she can tell Sofina Nightly what a great guy Billy is, how kind and funny, and how they're going to get married, and how she and Billy have so much to live for. And that if they kill him, it's like killing her too. And she's innocent and they can't condemn an innocent person to death. So there. They can't kill Billy either.

To her left, a short, pale, carroty-haired policeman is checking her out. Either he likes her, or is suspicious, or both. She wheels on him. "What's the split, Red?"

"Stay behind the line."

"I will, if you tell what the split is in there?" She points at the building.

"Someone might've taken hostages. We're checking it out."

Has Billy taken hostages? That doesn't sound like him. "What's his name? The guy who took the hostages."

"How do you know it's a he?"

"I watch a lot of vids. Hostage takers are always men."

"Actually, women have been making great strides in hostage taking in the last few years. But I'm not supposed to say anything."

"Then you probably weren't supposed to tell me there were hostages inside either, were you, Red? But I know that already." He looks over her shoulder, as if pretending to do some real police work. "I can find out whatever I want, anyway, in, like, ten seconds." She flashes her eCatt.

His eyes slide down to hers. "It's the serial killer, Billy the Goat. He was supposed to be executed tonight, but he escaped, and we think he might be holding people hostage."

"You going to shoot him?"

He shrugs. "Easier that way."

She knew it. All these police are trying to kill Billy in any way they can. It's like they're obsessed with him. And here's Red trying to seem all tough. He doesn't care one way or another about Billy, and she has a strong urge to tell him to check out the avalanching vids on *WeUs*, and maybe do some actual *police work* of his own. He might get a thrill knowing that he's talking to the woman who's been seen having sex by over a million people.

"I live in the building. I need to get in."

"No one in, and we vet everyone who comes out. Not that the Goat will be hard to recognize with his big ears and blue hair."

She recalls from an old police vid that when being investigated it's smart to ask questions that you already know the answers to. "He dyed his hair *blue*?"

"Yeah. The guy's got ears the size of an elephant's and a biochip in him and he thinks changing the color of his hair will throw us off. What an idiot."

"He can't be that big of an idiot if he escaped though, can he?"

Red waves her away. A formation of police drones whizzes over their heads and ascends into the haze of smoke and balconies. As Red follows the crafts upward, she ducks under the yellow police tape and runs behind the Fugitive Task Force van. The rear door of the van is open and there are cops inside, clicking and snapping their weapons and getting ready for an assault.

She drops down and looks around. Red seems to be fascinated by the disappearing drones and, frankly, doesn't seem to be the swiftest redhead she's ever met. In front of her, across eight feet of bare sidewalk, is a StarBuzz coffee-cannabis shop with the front door slightly ajar, as if people left in a hurry. The policemen in the van are still getting ready for their assault and the ones in the street are staring at the drones, so she darts in a crouch through the door. She crawls behind the counter and sits on the floor beneath a large THC smoothie blender. She waits to see if anyone saw her, but doesn't hear anything.

There's a door inside the shop that must lead into the building, but it's across thirty feet of exposed floor, with only a few small tables for cover. She takes a quick look at her eCatt: 2.6 million views. They've gone double avalanche! She suppresses a scream by biting her lip. Now more than ever, she needs to get Billy out, for love, for money, for fame, and in order that she never returns to the living dead at the Porker or anywhere else. *Double* avalanche. Most people go their whole lives and never even get to single.

It's now or never. She lies on her stomach and slithers across the floor, avoiding chair and table legs. The floor is grittier than it looks and smells of coffee, pot, and something that might be urine. She hits a chair with her ankle and it screeches. For a full minute she doesn't move, her cheek resting on a brownish stain while she inhales the pee-like smell. No one is coming. She starts again, crawling faster this time, and makes it to the door.

She pushes lightly on the bottom. It's not locked. Another foot and she's able to slide through, into the empty condominium hallway. The elevator is halfway down the hallway. Even closer, not more than fifteen feet away, is a door marked 'STAIRS.'

She pops to her feet and sprints toward the stairs. She slams into the STAIR door with her shoulder like she's seen in a thousand vids. It flings opens and she's bounding up the stairway three steps at a time. Halfway up the first flight, she turns the corner, breathing hard. Another three steps. Then another. She turns the next corner onto a small landing and is tackled. She crumbles beneath the weight, her hat and sunglasses sliding across the floor.

"Don't move!"

38

"I've got a plan."

Bassia looks at Rex, who seems captivated by the bottles in the medicine cabinet and then at Urban, who, she keeps noticing, is not bad looking at all. His chiseled, baked veneer makes him look more like a terra-cotta statue than an aging surfer. He seems to have wiry strength in his back and arms, which she can't see, but senses is there.

"I'm going to need your help." She lifts the shower nozzle off the wall bracket and extends it out so that the connecting hose is fully extended. She unscrews the hose from the wall and steps out of the bathtub with the showerhead and hose. "Sooner or later, the Goat will come back to the bathroom to get us. We'll need to take him out when he does."

"Won't that be dangerous?" Rex says.

Until this point, he's been staring into that medicine cabinet with a lover's eyes and it's quite possible he has a problem. Or else he's extremely nervous and can't handle the situation. Either way, it seems like he'll be of little help.

"Is it more dangerous than letting a serial killer do whatever he wants with us?" she says. "He's already started shooting."

"Let's do it," Urban says. As she nods at him, she thinks that his sinewy strength might come in handy.

"The bathroom door opens out," she explains. "If we tie this hose across the bottom, just a few inches above the ground, then when the Goat walks into the bathroom, he'll trip, and we can jump him."

"What if his gun goes off?" Rex asks.

"If you're scared you can lie down in the tub, that's the safest place."

He looks at the tub and actually seems to consider the possibility, but he doesn't move.

"We need to save my wife," he says eventually.

She nods. He seems to be coming around. "And ourselves as well," she says.

Urban goes to his knees and inspects the doorjamb. "There's nothing to attach the hose to," he says. He rolls toward the sink and opens the drawer beneath it. He removes an old hairbrush, inspects it, and then puts it back. He does the same thing with a toilet plunger. He stands and looks into the shower.

"We only need him to fall, right?" he says. "One way or another."

Bassia nods and Urban takes a bottle of Verdant Glory shampoo from the ledge and squeezes a small amount of avocado-like goo onto his fingers. He rubs them together and looks at Bassia.

"I like the way you think," she says.

Urban squeezes the shampoo at the bottom of the door. He rubs his fingers against the floor and then goes to the sink and fills a glass with water. He gets back on his knees and then slowly spills the water onto the shampoo and rubs it until the floor beneath the door is an eighteen inch spill of slick, green messiness.

Bassia smiles to herself. He's not only handsome but resourceful. "We'll need a weapon of some sort," she says. "So if the Goat goes to the ground we can get him."

"If only we had the Taser," Rex says

"What Taser?"

"I mean 'a'," he says. "If only we had *a* Taser."

"I've got it," Urban says. He's a man with answers and, right now, there's no one Bassia'd rather be stuck in the bathroom with.

He opens the medicine cabinet and removes two of the shelves, which are made of thick, opaque glass. He wraps each one with a hand towel and goes to the tub.

"Okay," he whispers. "On three, Bassia, you flush the toilet and Rex, you start coughing very loudly. Understand ..."

Urban waits for their consent and begins to count, "One, two, three."

At the moment that she flushes the toilet and Rex coughs, Urban smashes the glass shelves against the side of the bathroom tub. The glass shatters into the tub but leaves a long, sharp, dangerous shard in each of Urban's hands.

As he mimes stabbing a man with each glass shard, Bassia thinks they just might get out of this alive.

39

Billy wanders the penthouse with the pistol stuffed into the back of his tight-fitting URPLE jeans.

The gun had been placed on the couch between them just a few minutes ago, and Sofina was tempted but resisted the urge to reach for it. She's never fired a gun, wouldn't even know how. Now isn't the time to figure it out.

Billy's pacing and seems nervous, which makes her nervous. She never answered his question about whether she'd stop his execution. Is it because she doesn't want to make a promise she can't keep? Is it because she's that honest, even at a time like this? Or is she waiting for him to release her husband and the others out of the bathroom?

He's stalling. Is he waiting for an answer or does he want to spend more time talking? He seems like the old Billy, but what does she know about him anymore? Ten years in prison will change anybody. And he *is* a convicted serial killer. And a cannibal. How'd that happen? He used to run cross country. Her curiosity gets the best of her.

"Billy, I know I shouldn't ask, but I have to know. You weren't a serial killer when we went out, were you?"

He shakes his head. "After ... allegedly."

He runs his hand over the back of the couch, and then tries to open the closet door. It's stuck, thank God. She'd have a difficult time explaining the sex animate inside. He sniffs near the closet, as if he smells something, and then walks to Rex's desk against the far wall. He opens the top drawer of the desk and pulls out the thick, yellowed manuscript.

"Are you a writer?"

"My husband. He's been working on an epic poem."

He pulls a half-inch of pages off the top and reads aloud:

'Pretentious?Moi?'
is the second shortest joke
if you're English,
or English enough
to understand the first:
'Venison's dear.'

He tosses the pages back into the drawer. "This guy's your husband?"

"I've got some taste in men, haven't I?"

She regrets it the instant she says it.

"What's that supposed to mean?" He says, and she can't tell if he's amused or offended.

She circles the couch and approaches the desk. Whatever he wants, she'd like to give it to him. He's shorter than she recalls and a little thicker around the middle, but he hasn't lost the devilish squint in his eyes. Despite the hostages in the bathroom and his alleged crimes, he's doing his best. She believes that. He's always done his best. She recalls his surge of pride when he was elected captain of the cross-country team.

Two eCatts vibrate on the desk, where Billy'd made everyone place them before locking them up in the bathroom. Just before he advised them that they were lucky they weren't in prison, because otherwise he'd have to do a full cavity search. She ponders the pain and humiliation of all those years that he experienced, while she was building a multibillion-dollar company. Such an abrupt, unpredictable departure from what they'd been, both of them.

"I did a lot of thinking about you in prison," he says. "Especially near the end. You'd be surprised how much you think about your first love in your last days."

She looks into his eyes. The distance between them slips away and they are just two people, kids really, former friends and lovers from a time when friends and lovers meant so much. Maybe he feels it too. And maybe this feeling, if strong enough, will level his resistance, will be the emotional pivot that makes him decide to turn himself in.

She goes to hug him, to give him the comfort he must've needed so desperately in these last days, to hug him like a mother, or sister, or girlfriend – but her feet knock against his and they stumble over the couch.

He's lying on top of her again, his chest pressing into hers as it did all those years ago in the PT Cruiser, and she's staring into eyes which haven't changed with their faces, their lips, only a whisper apart. She kisses him, a quick, significant peck on his left cheek.

"I can hire a new attorney for you, Billy. I can get you the best criminal lawyer in the country. But you have to turn yourself in."

40

An accumulation of anxiety colonizes Rex's mind, like insects or early American settlers.

It feels inevitable, unstoppable, man-infest destiny. He opens the medicine cabinet again. To check. Just to see. He strokes the bottles one by one, a warm finger over the cool plastic exterior. His mouth waters.

There's a bottle in the back he hasn't seen before: AMAZALINE[20]. It must be Sofina's and is undoubtedly a mood enhancer with a name like that. Is she depressed? Of course she is. Everyone's depressed, but she's always managed to keep it squashed beneath her ambitions. Maybe she can't do it anymore, if this bottle is any indication. Maybe she's unhappy, which is the leading cause of divorce – as is the sudden return of old boyfriends.

Would she ever divorce him?

Of course she would.

He'd divorce himself if he could.

He will resist the AMAZALINE, despite the name. The best thing would be for him to enter a comatose state and

---

20 Side effects of AMAZALINE include blockages of the tear duct, nose, ear, rectum, and urinary passages; the inability to sneeze, burp, spit, clear nasal passages, and pass gas; as well as instant death.

wake up three months later in a hospital, free and clear of all the drugs in his bloodstream – and to discover whether he'll spend the rest of his life in prison. He looks at Urban, who's talking to Bassia. Are they flirting? He's never watched Urban flirt before, and it's not a pretty sight. His toothy smile looks like it causes pain.

The two of them have become watch guards, standing on opposite sides of the door, each holding a towel-wrapped shard of glass like a sword.

"Don't you worry about the radioactivity in the ocean when you surf?" Bassia says to Urban.

"That's part of it," he says. "The goal is to tap into the energy of the ocean, wherever it comes from and what-ever it is, the tides, the storms, the fish, and even the radiation, and then harness all that and take it for a ride. It's all about connecting, paddling out into the ocean and connecting with it and then leaving it as you found it for the next time. It's swallowed too much of my life, to be honest, but the thing is, sometimes, with the right wave, the right day, there's something profound in it, some-thing spiritual. Meaninglessly meaningful, if that makes any sense."

"It does. Maybe you can teach me one day," Bassia says. "If we ever get out of this."

"I'd like that. A lot."

Rex rolls his eyes. It's like watching two people swipe right or left at each other. Is it the prospect of imminent death that makes them so attractive to one another? Or is it something more genuine?

Focus. He needs to focus. What's his biggest concern? The body or Sofina's ex-boyfriend? The ex-boyfriend prob-ably, since he may kill them all. The less immediate threat is the body and that Rex may spend the rest of his life in a prison cell next to Billy – Sofina's two murderous exes playing cards and shooting the jailhouse breeze until their clocks run out. What would be *his* nickname? Rex the Taserex with Billy the Goat?

Is he being sarcastic?

To himself?

Is that even possible?

Sarcasm is an evolutionary skill and the inability to understand it can be evidence of damage to your parahippocampal gyrus. How does he even know this? And why is he using his hippocampus to retain it? There must've been something in the GLIDERALL that set his mind racing. Would AMAZALINE counteract that effect?

"Do you like being attorney general?" Urban asks. "It's an awful lot of work, I imagine."

Rex doesn't think he's ever seen Urban show this much interest in anyone else before. He wishes Urban would stop his excruciating smiling.

"Too much work to be honest. It's swallowed too much of my life too." She smiles.

"Why do you do it?"

"It's not that I like doing it so much. It's that I can't stand the thought of anyone else doing it. I pursue a lot of wrongful conviction cases where other attorneys general would be afraid to do so. Sometimes I can set an innocent person free. That keeps me going."

"The injustice. That's what bothered me too."

Rex could almost vomit listening to them, as they stand there like swordsmen and make googly eyes at each other. Actually, it wouldn't be such a bad idea to empty his stomach. As he shifts toward the toilet, the bathroom door bursts open, smacking him on the butt. He's about to protest when he sees Billy the Goat himself, standing back from the doorway, two feet away from the shampoo slime on the floor, and just out of reach of Urban's and Bassia's broken glass weapons.

41

Petty sits at a small table in the building manager's office on the bottom floor of Sofina Nightly's building.

Two police officers sit across from her, one is the carroty-haired guy who she talked to outside the building and the other is a square-shaped middle-aged woman, who looks like she's never laughed in her life. In the hallway there are even more policemen with guns, rifles, vests, drones, robots, monitors, and what looks like grenades. They're everywhere, these cops, with guns and weapons.

Have they even met Billy? All they need to do is talk to him.

She rubs her sore wrists. They didn't have to handcuff her, and the left one was too tight until Red finally removed it. Now, he stares at her like a gingerbread man, saying nothing. And she says nothing back to him. The room smells like coffee and donuts, which figures.

The square woman sits down across from her. It's clear that she's the superior officer, which isn't surprising since Red isn't the brightest rooster. "I'm Sargent Cindy Delgado." The woman extends her hand but Petty doesn't take it. "What's your name?"

"Am I under arrest?" She learned in a vid somewhere that when being interrogated, it's always good to answer a question with a question.

"Not yet. Name?"

"Why'd you handcuff me then?"

"We can find your name easily enough."

"Can you?"

"Are you going to keep doing that?"

"Am I?" It is getting a little old. "Okay, my name is Amy Jameson."

Red glances at her and then speaks her name into his eCatt.

"Why were you trying to enter the building?" Delgado asks.

"Like I told Red, I live here."

"Name's O'Malley," Red says, as if anyone cares. "Daniel O'Malley."

Delgado looks at her doubtfully, and Petty realizes that if they don't already know she doesn't live here, they will soon enough. "What's your unit number?"

"Do I need a lawyer?"

Delgado raises a single eyebrow. Red coughs behind her.

"Look, I don't live in the building, okay? I just said that so Red would let me in, but he didn't."

"It's O'Malley."

Delgado glances back at Red, who buries his head in his eCatt. "Most people would want to get as far away from here as possible."

"Do I look like most people?"

"I guess not."

"I'm visiting a friend."

"What's your friend's name?"

"You're big on names aren't you?"

"Do you work?"

"Do I?"

"Please, Ms. Jameson, make this easy."

"I've worked at the Pork & Drones Depot for the past 8 years." In vids, when someone lies, they always add in as much truth as they can.

"I've never met anyone who works in retail before. Must be interesting" Delgado's acting all friendly all of a sudden, but Petty can see right through that.

"It's not."

"Do you enjoy dealing with the public?"

"They suck."

"Okay, I see how this is going to go. Tell us your friend's name, the one who lives in this building?"

Petty looks from Delgado's dark eyes into Red's pale blue ones. They think they've got her, but they're wrong. "Sofina Nightly," she says and almost laughs when she sees the surprise on their faces.

"How do you know Mrs. Nightly?" Delgado looks skeptical.

"She came into the store one day. You know, the retail store, the *interesting* one with the *public* inside. We started talking and became friends. She's nice."

"You know what her job is?"

"Uh huh." Petty leans back in her chair. "Do you?"

Delgado signals to Red, and they both walk away. They must be checking on Sofina Nightly, maybe calling her, trying to figure out if Petty is her friend. But if Billy has taken Nightly hostage then there's no way they can find that out. She takes out her eCatt and does a search for the building, The Colonnade in San Francisco. Instantly there's a headline that says the escaped serial killer Billy the Goat is here and probably holding Sofina Nightly hostage, among others.

Unable to stop herself, she checks on the number of views of her vid on *WeUs*: 3.6 million. If she and Billy ever get out of here, they'll be rich and famous AF.

Red walks back into the room. "We're going to let you go, Ms. Jameson. We have too much going on to worry about someone like you." She starts to speak but Red raises a pinkish finger. "You're lucky. So don't talk and don't call me Red. Just go."

She knows she should take his advice, but she can't help herself. She was never good at taking advice. "Okay, but what does this Billy the Goat look like anyway? Just in case I, like, see him or something. I've heard he's handsome. Is he?"

"See for yourself. Believe it or not, the guy livestreamed a vid having sex."

"No way! Have you seen it?"

"Not yet." Which means he intends to. She wishes she could see his face when he does, when he learns who he's been talking to.

"What kind of woman would have sex with a serial killer?" This is too much fun. "Is she pretty? I bet she's really pretty."

"That's not what I heard. She's not like a model or a LuvMate or anything. We're calling her Just Above Average."

She grits her teeth. Who do they think they are? "So compared to a model or a sex animate, she's *just* above average? Maybe you cops need to get out more often and see what real people look like. They're not so attractive, you know. Ever been to the Department of Motor Vehicles?"

"This is why I told you not to talk. C'mon ..."

He leads her out of the office and into the hallway where all the cops, guns, robots, and ammunition are. It looks like a small army. An older policeman with a skunk-like streak of white in his hair walks past. He glances at her, then turns and looks again.

"Wait," he says. "That's her. That's Just Above Average!"

42

Rex exits the bathroom after Urban and Bassia and slips on the puddle of Verdant Glory shampoo on the floor.

His left foot shoots out from under him in a military-style kick. As he tries to recover his balance, his right leg kicks out and catches up to the left one. He goes airborne, and for a miraculous instant, he's parallel to the floor, levitating like a magician's assistant before dropping to the ground with a deadened *thump*.

The Goat points his gun at him. "What're you—? I mean, quiet down. Get up!"

"Rex, are you okay?" Sofina asks.

He nods. He places his hands to the side of the spill to support himself and slices his left thumb on one of the glass shards that was left behind. Sucking the blood from his thumb, he meekly walks from the bathroom and lines up next to Urban against the wall. As he stands there, it's not only his back and knees that hurt but now his thumb and tailbone as well. His head is heavy and fuzzy from the fall, the events of the day, the alcohol, or the drugs. He smells like a rainforest and can feel the shampoo slowly seeping through the seat of his pants.

The only good thing is Sofina appears to be fine. She's standing on the other side of the couch and doesn't seem nervous at all. Which is odd. She should be nervous. How can she *not* be nervous? The pistol looks like a bazooka in the Goat's hand, and perhaps even more disconcertingly it doesn't look like he's used to holding one.

"There's no way out, Billy," Bassia says. "Give yourself up." She's standing on the other side of Urban and seems determined to aggravate the Goat.

"Quiet down."

Was he like this in high school? Rex wonders. Saying 'quiet down' all the time? What did Sofina ever see in him?

"You still have a chance, Billy," Bassia says. "Otherwise, they're going to kill you. First chance they get."

Rex doesn't understand why she keeps at this.

"They were going to kill me anyway," Billy says. "So what difference does it make?"

"After midnight, there will be no more executions in the United States," Bassia softens her tone. "She's good, Rex realizes, now that he understands what she's doing. "It's the new law. You were supposed to be the last one. Don't you remember? If you give yourself up, you'll live to a ripe old age. Otherwise…"

"I don't believe you. Everyone's lied to me from the beginning."

Rex isn't sure if he believes her either. Wouldn't there be some exception for someone who escaped? Either way, Rex hopes that whatever happens, it happens soon. The shampoo has oozed through his pants and into his underwear. His ass is starting to itch.

"It's true," Sofina says. "You're safe, Billy, and you know you can't shoot them anyway. They're my friends."

Rex wants to say that he's more than a *friend* but doesn't interject. He figures his best chance right now is making himself invisible and covertly scratch his ass.

"Give me the gun, Billy," Bassia says.

"You can trust her, Billy," Sofina says.

"Okay, okay." The Goat rotates from the people lined up against the wall to Sofina and back again. As he revolves, Rex notices how large his ears are; it's like he's a blue-haired owl or something. Were those ears part of his appeal to Sofina? Did they have something to do with his becoming a serial killer?

"I'll make a deal," the Goat says. "If you all agree, I leave and no one gets hurt."

Bassia takes a small step forward. "Tell us what you want, Billy."

"Let me go. Don't come after me. Don't try to kill me."

"Nobody in this room will follow you."

He thinks about this. "No, I don't want *anyone* to come after me. Ever. Not the police or the FBI or the military or the Fugitive Task Force or anybody. I'm no threat. Never have been. Ask Sofi. Aren't there enough things that you all have to deal with right now? Like the wildfires and the ocean and stuff? And unemployment and all those unhappy people? So just let me go. I'll leave the country and you'll never hear from me again. Deal?"

Urban nudges Rex's foot and Rex almost jumps off the ground. He didn't realize how edgy he is. Rex attempts to cover his sudden movement by scratching his ankle with the opposite shoe, which almost makes him fall. The Goat sees it.

"Quiet down," The Goat says. "What's going on?"

"Nothing," Urban says.

"I saw you move." The Goat points at Rex.

"Cramp."

The Goat looks back at Sofina and smiles. "Guess it runs in the family."

Is that a joke, a private joke between *them*? For a terrible instant, Rex believes that they must've had sex when he was locked in the bathroom. Sofina gets frequent cramps in her calves, but how does the Goat know this? Is that why the Goat came here in the first place? Why he locked everyone but Sofina in the bathroom? Because he wanted to have sex with her one more time before he dies? Rex's had enough, enough of Urban and Bassia and Sofina and Billy, enough of his knees and back and thumb, enough of Tasers and dead bodies and prescription drugs, enough of this whole, long, painful, tragic, stupid day.

"You mean, *my* family, Goat? The family that consists of Sofina and me and *not* you," he says. "Because we're the family and what runs through *us*, or in *us* or whatever, is *our* business and *our* business alone."

The Goat squints at him. As if Rex is the crazy one. As if Rex was the one who had killed and eaten all those people. "Quiet down," he says and then turns back to Sofina, as if to ask what is wrong with Rex, her husband.

When the Goat is looking the other way, Urban touches Rex's arm and nods toward the sliding door that leads to the terrace. Rex looks outside and can barely make out through the thick smoke the outline of a police drone, hovering in place. Rex remembers that he'd left the door open to try and cover the smell of the body with smoky air. Now he sees through that same crack, the drone aiming its rifle-like weapon at the back of the Goat's head.

43

"You call *me* Just Above Average?" Petty says. "Most of you cops could play the extras in a zombie vid. No need for make-up."

She sits in the same chair at the same table in the same manager's office. It seems that no matter what she does, she ends up back in the same place, in the same job, watching the same vids, talking to the same cops. Her life, on endless repeat.

On the other side of the room, Delgado and Red are watching the vid of Billy and her. Occasionally Red will raise his head and glance her way. He either wants her, which is not happening, or he's trying to make her feel embarrassed, which she's not.

"How many views?" she says. "That's all I want to know."

Delgado looks at her for the first time in a while. "Does that matter, Ms. Petty Kowalski Manriquez? We know you lied about your name."

"It's the *only* thing that matters."

Delgado returns to the vid. When it ends, Petty hears Billy's long, deep satisfied groan and smiles. Delgado takes a thoughtful sip of coffee.

"Did you know Billy Wharton was an escaped convict when you recorded this video?"

Petty doesn't respond. She's done responding. Who are they to call her Just Above Average when they're all *below* average. Above Average would've been fine, if they'd left it at that. But the 'just' means that she barely crosses average. Billy said she's the most beautiful woman he's ever seen, and they think she's *just* above average, and now they want her help to get him. Not happening.

"Did you know he was an escaped convict when you recorded this?" Delgado repeats. "He's tagged as Billy 'The Goat' Wharton? So you must've known."

"Is that his name?"

"You should know. You tagged him."

Delgado's trying to trick her, but Petty's onto her. "*WeUs* tags people automatically."

"But you've obviously been checking the views, so you must've known at some point."

She'll have to be careful here. But as long as she doesn't admit to knowing who Billy is or that he escaped, she'll be okay. She can have sex with anyone she wants, and can livestream herself whenever she wants. That's what America stands for. That's democracy. That's freedom.

"You haven't answered my question," Delgado says, using her stern voice now. Probably she's jealous of Petty and Billy and all their views.

"Because you didn't answer mine."

Delgado shakes her head. "I don't think you fully understand. If you are convicted for harboring a fugitive—"

"Is that what you guys call it? *Harboring?* What's he, like, an aircraft carrier?"

"It is a crime to harbor or conceal any known fugitive. Your responsibility was to report him to the police as soon as you knew he was a fugitive."

"I livestreamed him on *WeUs*. How is that harboring or concealing? I did better than report him, I *broadcast* him."

"Ms. Manriquez, what is your relationship with Billy Wharton?"

Petty looks at her and then at Red and can't help herself. "We're engaged to be married."

"What?" Red says. "When did this happen?"

Delgado flips through Billy's file on her desk. "There's nothing in his file about him being married or engaged, and that would have been important information given that he was going to be executed."

"It happened today. I met him at the Porker and we hit it off and got engaged right after we livestreamed ourselves." She glares at Red. "He thinks I'm beautiful."

"Well, he's been on death row for ten years, looking at old, naked men all day, so..."

"What have you been looking at, Red? Farm animals?"

"It's O'Malley."

Delgado clears her throat. "The question is, Ms. Manriquez, did you know he was a fugitive when you first livestreamed this?"

Petty sees how she keeps coming around to the same question, the one she should never answer. But she's not as dumb as Delgado thinks. "You haven't told me how many views?"

"Over two million," Delgado says. "Now answer my question."

Petty sits up. "I'm going to be rich."

"That's a good thing because lawyers are expensive." Delgado turns to Red. "Book her for harboring a fugitive."

"What?" Petty's not a criminal.

She's rich.

She's famous.

She has a fiancé.

It's so unfair. Just when her dreams are coming true. When she's met a man she loves and who loves her, when she's found a way to make money and get away from the endlessly undead days at the Porker. Just when she's going to learn how to make really cool vids, with unusual camera angles and moody music, enter into the future she'd been waiting for all her life. And now that it's here, now that she's finally free and alive and loved, they want to arrest her, to turn her into a zombie again.

"But he thinks I'm fun and interesting and, like, beautiful," she says and drops her head on the table so that they won't see the tears in her eyes.

44

The Goat looks nervous.

He's shaking, his eyes are darting back and forth, and he could well be on the verge of a breakdown. That's what Bassia thinks as she stands against the wall. She'd charge him herself, but she's spotted the armed drone hovering just beyond the terrace, aiming through the crack in the door and waiting for a clear shot. The problem is that the Goat is standing directly between the hostages and the drone. And John Missionary or whoever is piloting won't risk a shot if it might take out one of them.

It's a stealthy drone that produces only a light whirring sound. Her task is to keep Billy distracted so he doesn't hear it while she gets the hostages out of the line of fire.

"Billy, listen to me. There's an easy way out of this."

"Quiet down!"

She pretends that his words scare her. She covers her face in fear and slides to her right, pushing into Urban who pushes into Rex. They shift a critical eighteen inches. Still in the line of fire, but in better shape. A few more of those and the drone will have a clear shot to take the Goat out.

"Billy, look at me. There's no way you can be executed, even if they catch you right now. Look at me. You're safe.

We'll help you. You can go back to prison and live out your natural life."

"Quiet down!"

She slides again and pushes them all another eighteen inches to the right. By her calculation, the drone will have a clear shot if she can do that one or two more times. Right now, it's Rex who seems reluctant to shift. He's sucking his bloody thumb and acting like his feet are stuck to the floor.

The outline of the drone becomes darker and more pronounced. Somewhere the pilot has seen what she's doing. The gentle whirr changes pitch as it comes closer. She reaches down as if to adjust her right shoe but falls slightly to the side and manages to nudge Urban another foot or so. But Rex, as usual, seems unaware of what's happening.

"Billy, please go. Please," Sofina says.

As Billy turns around to see Sofina and possibly the drone, Bassia takes a large step forward. "What'd you do with the governor, Goat? Did you kidnap him? Where is he? Underground? In a basement?"

The Goat spins back. "How do I know?"

"You killed him!" The drone flies over the terrace to the window. The whirr increases.

"What? I didn't do anything to him. I was in jail. Quiet down!"

"After you escaped."

"I don't even know what the guy looks like. Sofina, tell them …"

There's a rumble out the terrace window that Bassia identifies as an earthquake, the one they've been warning about.

The Goat turns around and sees the drone.

Bassia pushes Urban into Rex and both tumble to the right as the Goat dives on the ground. The building trembles as a shot rings out, whizzing through the room and thwacking to a stop.

Bassia leaps on top of the Goat. In a flash, Urban is with her on the floor. As Bassia wrestles the pistol from the Goat's hand, Urban locks a forearm beneath his chin. Rex grabs the pistol as it slides toward him.

Urban puts the Goat in a chokehold and slowly closes the wedge of his right arm on the Goat's neck. Bassia has the Goat's arms from behind. Her eyes meet Urban's. They make a good team. The Goat grunts and squirms but she doesn't loosen her grip. Urban continues to squeeze. The Goat's face goes from red to white.

"Everybody all right?" she asks.

Rex and Sofina nod silently.

Incredibly, no one was shot, not even the Goat, who has stopped squirming. Bassia looks to see where the bullet landed. She glances back at the terrace to where the drone is still hovering and traces the direction of its shot.

Just as she hears the police outside the front door, she sees it: a splintered, quarter-sized hole in the bottom half of the closet door.

A tremor pulses through the building. The penthouse rattles and shakes.

From the Desk of Sofina Nightly

June 16, 2029

The problem is not only the degradation of our land, sea, and air but our moral and spiritual ~~failure~~ impoverishment.

We need a new enlightenment, a judicious ~~and~~ yet fearless reassessment of our values, culture, customs, and institutions.

(naïve? maybe it has to be. maybe that's the point.)

Our generation and the generations prior have been irresponsible ~~citizens~~ caretakers, not only of the planet, but also of our collective souls.

(souls? is there a better word? avoid accusatory tone?)

It's a new age + we need a ~~nobler worthier~~ more honorable way of placing ourselves on the planet. Requires new definitions, new ethics, new rights, new organizing principles.

To be reassessed/redefined: freedom, equality, justice, democracy, capitalism, the inalienable rights of everyone and everything, etc.

The more that rights are extended (genders, workers, races, reli-

gions, nationalities, animals, etc.) the ~~better~~ more moral our society becomes. Always true.

Not only do we need to extend rights given to animals, but to grant rights to the environment (earth?) as well. Note: not more environmental rights for people, rights for the environment. The environment (earth) ~~owned~~ managed as a transnational trust for ~~future generations~~ itself?

    (animals included environmental trust)

My commitment: 100% of wealth + time + energy
Save California.
Save country.
Save planet/ourselves.
Stay strong.
Believe!

Part IV

11:04 PM
June 16, 2029

45

B illy lies sideways on the sheet-less bed.

Bent at the waist, hands folded, bare heels high against the wall, and head hanging down. It's a familiar position in which he's spent a large part of the last ten years of his life. He's a prisoner again, but without anger, pity, or despair, just disappointment. He ignores the coughs and snores from the nearby cells as he breathes slowly and steadily in the darkness. In and out.

"Breathing in time.

Lemon and lime.

Rhythm and rhyme."

They returned him to the same cell with the same stainless-steel toilet and same porthole window, the same thin cracks in the ceiling, and the same old stench of plaster and disinfectant. His 6` x 9` tuna-can castle, with enough room to sit, stand, and lie, enough space for push-ups, jumping, and stretching, enough for any man. No limitations except his own.

He'd inquired about the two guards who'd escorted him to the execution chamber earlier this morning – the unconscious ones he'd dragged behind the driverless van – and was relieved to find out that they were fine. They'd been taken to the hospital for smoke inhalation and dehydration but have since been released. They'd asked the warden to express their gratitude to Billy for not abandoning them where they might've died. He's grateful for their gratitude and grateful for the chance to feel grateful, because that's how gratitude works. It feeds on itself.

The other death row inmates hooted at his blue hair when he was escorted back to his cell. He'd hooted back, smiled, and bumped fists. They'll want to know all about his escape, and he'll tell them some things, but not all. He won't tell them that he had sex – no, made love – with a beautiful, blue-haired woman that he intends to marry. Not right away. And he won't tell them that he drank fine boxed wine and smoked killer weed and even reconnected with an old girlfriend. They know life has sped up on the outside but could never imagine how much. It'd be cruel to let them know. How could he explain that you can now live a lifetime in a few hours? So he won't tell them that. And he won't tell them about Petty.

His friend.

His lover.

His fiancée.

Incredibly, there'd been another woman as well. What was her name? With all the random facts? Sally. Only she wasn't a real woman. She was a sex animate with splendid espresso nipples. He'll tell the other inmates about her, only he'll make her a real human. Otherwise they might think that he's not only a cannibal, but a pervert too. And one of those labels is enough for any man. So he'll lie about that. He'll tell them how he took her three, no, four times by the side of the high-way in every possible position. And how she begged for more.

He'll tell them about the flocks of bird-like drones in the sky, the self-driving cars, and that people livestream pornos of themselves like vacation photos. He'll tell them that the environment is worse, far worse, than they can imagine, and that if they don't get out soon, there will be nothing left to get out to.

Petty. His thoughts keep returning to Petty. Where is she now? Where could she possibly be?

The jeep is fully charged, and Petty has over 28,000 Euro-Dollars in accessible *WeUs* credits in her account as she descends into the valley.

She's owed another 200 EDs from the ponytailed guy who assaulted her in the Porker. Not that she'll bother to collect. She and Billy are already 19+ Avalanche on *WeUs*. Over nineteen million people have seen her having sex. That's exciting and a little scary too. She rubs her hands up her thighs, over the sides of her stomach and then hugs herself. Soon she'll be making more money in a day than she did in a month at the Porker.

She rolls down the window and squints into the blackened breeze. The wind catches the blue hair on the side of her head and flaps it like a dog's ear. It feels free and fun and makes her want to bark. If only the state wasn't burning down and the ocean rising and all that. She never cared about that stuff when she was at the Porker, even sort of welcomed it. Because any change is a good change when you're unhappy. That's the thing about happiness: Happy people don't want things to change and unhappy people do.

Is everyone unhappy?

Because she doesn't think she is, not anymore. She's famous and making money and has a great boyfriend, even if he's stuck in jail. But they met, that's the important thing, so, yeah, she's happy.

Is this what happiness feels like? She thought there'd be, like, more to it.

She cruises between hill fires and smokes what's left of Billy's Old's Kool cannabis. The jeep rattles as if going over railroad tracks, but the road is smooth. The jeep has been due for repairs for over a year now and that's probably it, what's causing the shakiness.

For all her snarky attitude, zombie vids, and smoking and drinking, she's actually had little adventure in her life. She's been trapped at the Porker without a boyfriend, money, or excitement for as long as she can remember. Maybe she's not what she thought she was. Maybe nobody is. She doesn't know what made her take Billy home and livestream them having sex. She'd done that twice before, but with people she knew better. Other than that though, she's been a zombie woman in a zombified life. They say people want to see characters like themselves in the vids they watch, so there you go.

It's been over three hours since Billy was recaptured. She hopes they haven't done anything to him.

Are they really going to get married? Why not? She's never really cared about a man before, never *really* cared, and certainly never actually said 'I love you' to anyone except during sex, which doesn't count.

Billy, Billy, Billy. She loves that name.

What does she know about love? All she's ever loved before is zombie vids and cannabized coffees. She knows about lust and lust is ice, especially if the person lusts you back. But lust isn't love. It's just fun. Love is different.

They say love is what you make it. Love is truth, they say also, which sounds ice, but doesn't really mean anything. Or truth is love, which sounds better, but means even less.

She's either going to puke, or there's an animal gnawing a hole in her stomach. She's afraid to turn on her eCatt, because of what she might hear. Maybe Billy's already been executed. That would be the worst. That would make her the most unhappy ever. She swallows something sour that burns as it goes down.

She'd screamed like a ghoul when she heard that someone had been shot in the penthouse, before anyone knew who it was. Then, after the longest ten minutes in her life, Red finally told her that Billy was alive. That somebody else had been shot by mistake, but he didn't say who. Maybe it was that Sofina chick, his ex-girlfriend. She deserves it. No, that's not right. She never did anything to Petty, except love the same man, and Petty can't blame her for that.

The police didn't let her see Billy when they took him away, but Red let her know that he was going back to San Quentin. Red said he didn't know if Billy'd still be executed or not. Nobody did.

Then Red and Delgado kept interrogating her in that stupid, gray room. By that time, they'd discovered that she didn't actually know Sofina Nightly and, more importantly, that Sofina Nightly didn't know her. But she stuck with her story like Billy had told her. And repeated it over and over.

No, she didn't know Billy was a serial killer.

She'd met him at the Porker, and they had great sex on *WeUs* is all.

She followed him to Sofina Nightly's building because she wanted to let him know how many million views they were getting.

They asked if she often had sex with strangers and she said no, because once you were having sex with someone they were no longer a stranger, were they?

Which was a good one.

Then they asked if she could show them other vids where she was having sex and she showed them the one with her old girlfriend, Janine. Only 242 views after three years, which was sad and nothing like the numbers with Billy. Janine looked pretty ice though.

And then they asked if she was a prostitute. She said it would be hard to be a prostitute if you were *just* above average, wouldn't it? It's not like any policemen would buy her, and everyone knows how much policemen like hookers and donuts. She said that though she isn't really sure if policemen actually like hookers that much. She was just mad. Red and Delgado glanced at each other but didn't say anything.

She didn't bother to tell them that it was the *just* that hurt her feelings. She was ice with being above average. Why did they have to hit her with the *just*? The more she thought about it, the more upset she got, until she finally asked for a lawyer. They thought she wanted the lawyer for their questions, but she actually just wanted to see if she could sue them for extortion or slander or whatever it's called when you say something mean about somebody.

Just above average.

Over 19 million viewers disagree.

Whatever, it worked, because not long after, they let her go. She got in her old jeep, set the *weDrive* for TLC Correction's San Quentin and here she is pulling into the prison parking lot.

Billy's feet, high on the cell wall, begin to go numb and the familiar tingling descends into his calves. This is the painful part, the part he has to get past, when the blood descends.

"Breathing in time…"

Of all the things on the outside, it's the women that the inmates will most want to hear about. Billy's certain about that. If Petty and Sally are any indication, they've become more confident, sexy and unashamed than any prisoner could possibly imagine. Women not only want sex as much as men, but pursue it as enthusiastically. To bust a quickie by the side of the road like Sally or broadcast a bumper to the world like Petty seems normal. Expected. Unremarkable.

Bold, bald, and sometimes blue, that's what women have become. Some so shockingly blue that he had trouble maintaining an erection. (He'll keep that to himself.) Then again, he's lived an entire lifetime in a day, and who can maintain an erection for an entire lifetime? What would that do to his blood pressure?

First, he'll discuss these things with Petty, even his impotence. He'll discuss everything with Petty. They have a lot to talk about, decades worth of conversation.

The state has stopped all executions, that's what he's been told. But the warden didn't know whether Billy would be grandfathered into his own death or not. "It'd be an ironic thing to be grandfathered into dying," the warden had said. Billy wasn't sure that ironic was the right word, but he didn't say anything. If it were possible to still execute him, the warden went on, then the decision would be the new governor's to make, the new governor named Sofina Nightly.

She never gave him an answer as to whether she'd execute him, though she did agree to hire him a good new attorney, which she's already done. His appeals have run out, but who knows? A new lawyer can't hurt. Billy just wishes he hadn't yelled 'quiet down' so much.

Sofi'd had a lot on her mind, what with him showing up at her penthouse and the governor getting shot in her closet – something which the police tried to pin on him. As if he had enough time in a single day to escape from jail, attempt sex with an animate, shop, shower, smoke, drink, make love to a real woman, livestream it, get engaged, reconnect with an old girlfriend, and then go kill the governor. Time moves fast in 2029, but not that fast.

The bed shakes; there's a shimmer in the cell walls.

Petty can't believe they actually *charge* for parking in a prison parking lot. The car stops and she flashes her eCatt without looking at the price; money doesn't matter anymore. When the jeep pulls inside, the signs overhead are swinging back and forth, and there's debris flying all around. Is this what prisons are like? The jeep jerks one way and then the other. She really needs to get it fixed.

She's not going back to the Porker whether Billy is alive, undead or, like, truly dead. That's decided. And she's going to try to stop smoking and drinking so much, and stop watching zombie vids, or at least slow down on them. Mostly she's going to try to do new things. Lifey things. Most people are zombies. Maybe the only person she's ever met who isn't completely undead, who is a total original, is Billy. That's so admirable, and maybe admiration is love.

Billy the Goat. Possible serial killer and cannibal and ... fiancé? She laughs as she recalls his erection wilting when he saw her blue pubes. Like boiled okra. Everything about him is cuddly and cute and hilarious and alive.

A car approaches in the opposite direction, cutting across the lanes in the parking lot and flashing its lights. What's the rush? She feels like cancelling the *weDrive*, yanking the wheel, and speeding for its headlights. She pictures her last moments, her arms locked against the wheel, her legs locked and braced. But no, she won't do it. What about the people in the other car? Who may have been visiting a serial killer of their own.

She saw a documentary once, maybe the only doc vid she's ever watched, that said that consciousness can't understand itself. In the same way that a murder mystery can't solve itself and needs people from the outside like an attractive CSI unit or an alcoholic detective. Maybe that's all she is: consciousness. All she has is the knowledge of herself by herself, which means she is something that she can never understand. She needs someone from the outside to do that, like Billy. Which means love is, like, self-knowledge from someone else, or something like that.

She'll never have sex with another man as long as she lives. That's decided. She knows that already. It doesn't make sense, but there it is. Billy Wharton will be her last male lover. She will allow herself women occasionally, perhaps, but not another man. Because the purpose of life is to prevent yourself from becoming zombified, and Billy does that for her. So she'll do this for him.

Day-to-day living will make you a zombie and she's been fighting it the wrong way with vids, sex, and drugs. The thing about being undead is that you don't realize it. It's like being in a coma. Five, ten years can pass and then you wake up and nothing's changed.

She will not be undead again.

So what if Billy killed nine people? He didn't mean it. She wishes she'd told him that she forgives him even if he did. She forgives him, and she'll try to forgive all the rest as well, all the people who'd created this soul-killing world and are themselves, without knowing it, zombies too.

The car parks near the surrounding wall of the prison building. There's a light on at the entrance and a glow in the guard towers, but that's all. It looks closed. She lies down in her seat to sleep and is sure of one thing: that love is the opposite of being undead. She places the eCatt on the holder in the middle of the dashboard and aims it at herself. She turns on the livestream so the world can watch her sleep. People like watching other people sleep, especially famous people like she is now. And when they do a location search and find she's sleeping outside Billy's prison, she'll probably go 10+ avalanche before morning.

The jeep shakes again, crazily, as if it's in a gigantoraptor's mouth. It bounces and smashes down. She bites her tongue, tastes a shot of blood. There must be something wrong with the jeep's suspension, except it's stopped. Why would it bounce when it's stopped? And lean to one side?

There's a guard tower on the opposite side of the building, its dim light rocking in the night sky. Only it's not just the tower, the entire prison is wobbling like a chunk of gray jello. There's a loud groaning and the thick wall in front of her begins to crumble and then split. As if ripped or something. A pause. Silence. The jeep rocks back and forth. And then a single white-shirted guard runs through the hole in the wall, followed by three orange jump-suited prisoners with a whole bunch more behind them.

She gets out of the car and walks toward the prison.

Billy goes deeper into his meditation.

Within him, he finds the unhealed wounds of his alleged victims, the eight or nine people he may or may not have killed. He can almost see their faces, but not quite, as if he's looking through a shower door. Preachers, counselors, therapists, priests, and parole officers have said that he needs to confess and seek forgiveness, with some claiming that the salvation of his soul depends on it. But it's dishonest to confess sins that you don't know if you committed, and God will understand that even if no one else does.

He contemplates those lost souls, nine of them, adds in the former governor as well, and then sends peace-filled thoughts to their families and loved ones through the greater cosmos. Does it do any good?

Who knows?

There's an old woman in Patagonia, who gets on her knees every morning and prays for the sun to rise. They say even she doesn't fully believe in what she is doing, but she doesn't dare stop. Does she do it because she loves the sun, the earth, or her children? Is she merely acknowledging the greater cosmic forces? Does it give her life meaning, even if the act itself is meaningless?

And yet... her fate, his fate, the fate of his alleged victims, is in the hands of greater cosmic forces. And in a great cosmic sense, what other forces are there?

A low rattle from the cells down the hall, the sound of books and pictures falling, the floor angling, and the air is electric. Whoops, claps, and laughter erupt from nearly every cell. Inmates cheer for quakes, fires, floods, and droughts. They cheer for mudslides, riots, and upheavals. They root for anything and everything to change. And right now anything and everything is quaking. They're hoping that this is it, the one that will crash California into the sea. He closes his eyes. Let it go. In and out.

Breathing in time.

Guilt and innocence.

Love and death.

Damnation and salvation.

Lemon and lime.

Rhythm and rhyme.

His bed clatters and slips. Dust falls. Cracking and crushing. The prison rocks and cleaves, tossing him from the bed. He opens his eyes on the cement floor, observes the cracking and compacting around him. He sits up in a puddle. The far wall of his cell is sliced open and there, in this chasm of freedom, he sees her, blue hair flapping, bowed legs backlit by the swaying spotlights of the parking lot.

And if these are his final breaths and this is his final sight, he will only be grateful, forever grateful.

Petty.

46

The interior of Urban's van consists of a mattress, a bean bag chair, a lamp, a table, a dusty surfing trophy, a small refrigerator, and a grill.

After they left Sofina's condo a couple of hours ago, Bassia and Urban avoided the reporters, cameras, and media drones, and slipped into a wine bar where they talked for more than an hour about surfing, art, and injustice. Then, ignoring the earthquake warnings and ongoing tremors, he invited her back to his home, this van. She's never been in the inside of a van before and can't conceive of living in one for any length of time, much less fifteen years. The problem isn't the lack of square footage. It's that she can't stand up. Then again, all she has to do is step outside, and what's so terrible about that?

The van smells like bubble gum, which Urban told her is surf wax. There's a Raphael print taped on the side wall, 'The School of Athens,' which she recognizes from an art-history class. There they are: Aristotle, Plato, Socrates, Diogenes, and Alexander the Great, among others, the classical giants of the Renaissance. It's the only personal item in the van – except for the trophy and the surfboard wedged against the far wall – and an odd choice for a man who seems more practical than philosophical, but maybe that's the point. She's not exactly sure where the van is parked, except that it's an isolated spot right next to the ocean.

The Goat has been returned to prison and it looks like Sofina will decide whether he'll be executed – if he still can be. If Bassia knows anything about Sofina, she won't pursue it. She's not one to put anyone to death, least of all an ex-boyfriend.

When did life become so incestuous and coincidental? How is it that in a state of 50 million souls, they all seem to know one another, all seem to be acting in a meta-digital farce with their exquisitely-timed entrances and exits, their offsetting logins and logouts, their alternating livestreams and data drops?

She sits on the mattress and stares at the Raphael. Alexander the Great once met Diogenes, the philosopher who lived on the streets of Athens and professed his poverty a virtue. Later, Alexander, the man who would go on to conquer most of the known world, would proclaim that if he were not himself, he would wish to be Diogenes. They were not so far apart.

As she is not so far from Urban.

She never knew where any of her fellow artists lived, the ones she used to share a square of sidewalk with at Fisherman's Wharf before they disappeared, but their homes can't be much different than this. Only less mobile. The surf and artistic undergrounds of San Francisco aren't so different, united by the uncommon pursuit of something other than comfort and approval. Some of them are selfish and listless, escapees rather than pursuers, sure, but some of them are the real deal. You know it when you see it.

If she were not Bassia Augustine, Attorney General of the State of California, then she might be the female, miming Urban McChen – who at this moment lies shirtless next to her, caressing her arm.

She places her hand on a tuft of salt-and-pepper hair in the middle of his chest, perfectly sculpted by a thousand surf sessions. She wants to want him and, letting herself go, does. And yet, she can't believe she's doing this when there is so much else to do.

He kisses her and asks, "Do you want to have sex with me?"

Her eCatt has been turned off. There's nothing and no one outside this van that can reach her. She's never been with a man like Urban before, who seems so – what? – contentedly and unapologetically impoverished? So monastic and athletic? So thickly ponytailed?

Yet there are so many problems with the governor's death, even in the preliminary report she read before she turned off her eCatt. Why was the governor epoxied in the Nightlys' closet? Something he, himself, would've been unable to do. Why does the preliminary autopsy conditionally say that the governor died of cardiac arrest, not the shot from the drone through the closet door? What about the welts and burn marks on the top half of his body, or the Taser stuck in the building's garbage chute?

And what about Urban, pecking her neck with gentle kisses and waiting for an answer?

"Very much," she says and lies back on the mattress.

He lifts her shirt and kisses her stomach. She arches into him. There's a slight breeze from the driver's window and she's cool against his mouth, warm against his body. He's weighty on top of her, smelling of ruggedness, sweat and must. She hasn't been with a man for a long time and has forgotten their heft, their coarseness. She leans one way and then the other beneath him, waiting and wanting.

"It was me," she says. "The mime you saw at Fisherman's Wharf. That was me."

He opens her shirt, button by button. There's an artfully-placed mole just below her clavicle and another on the slope of her left breast. Can she feel him shaking? Is it because she's the attorney general, or the crazy events of this day, or something more?

Another button on her shirt, and he can't decide if he wants to hurry or slow down. He's aware of his breathing and remembers what he's forgotten about desiring and wanting to be desired: the in-betweenness of it, the unknowingness, the reciprocal otherness.

He's never had a partner, wife, or child and wonders if that's not so much a choice as a consequence. With Bassia, this exquisite and powerful woman, he senses the risk, the fear. Because this thing that's happening between them feels authentic, consequential even though they've never been surfing or shared a meal. If only he knew what exactly this thing is.

Another two buttons and her shirt falls away. She pulls her arms loose and raises her bright eyes to his as he cups the sides of her breasts snugly into his palms. He slides his hands from her breasts, running them lightly down her sides, and removes her skirt. He rolls to the side and takes a long look at the pretty oval of her face, her bald head, her long neck, teasing breasts, and the sleek slope of her stomach with its salty sweet heat.

An image of the governor in the bathtub flashes in his mind. Is that why he's shaking? Is that what's making him so nervous? There's no getting over his responsibility, though the emotion of it seems far away. It's all those years of working death penalty cases. Has he been too close to death and gotten used to it? Far too many innocent men have died and the governor is just one more. He was no better than any of them, the last among unequals. There's a good chance that Urban will never feel anything more about his death than he does now. Maybe there's something wrong with him. There's no way to know.

"I knew it was you," he says. "There's only one woman with eyes like yours."

He slides down her stomach, trailing his tongue and gently, slowly spreading her legs.

She leans back and thinks *this* needs to be a priority. More of *this*, which has no greater purpose than closeness, responsiveness, and pleasure. The people's justice can wait. But can she? Despite herself, her thoughts circle back.

Everyone in the Nightlys' penthouse is a suspect, including Sofina, including herself. The police will do their investigation, come up with a suitable narrative, but to what end? There was an errant drone shot during a tremor. No one's to blame. There will be the subsequent report which will highlight the irregularities, the inconsistencies, and this will catch some interest in the media. By the next day, it will be yesterday's news, and by the next largely forgotten.

People will seek closure like they always do, not truth, not justice. It'll be enough that the Goat was recaptured and the hostages safe. The governor died, but it was an unfortunate accident, nothing more. The incestuous nature of modern existence has its advantages, and Californians, like all Americans, expect coincidence. They're suspicious when it doesn't occur.

She's suddenly tired of all that, tired of reckonings and retribution, tired of the arbitrary laws of the State of California. Tired of the busyness in her own mind.

She stares at the sloped roof of the van and concentrates on the man beneath her, the throbbing between her thighs. She reaches down to his head and is surprised to find in her left hand a fistful of ponytail, which she grabs and drives him into her as the van begins to sway and rise above the ground.

Urban feels her tremble. She pitches his head in cadence with her hips. He's tossed against her thigh as the van lists to the right. Did something hit them? She doesn't seem to have noticed, only grips his head tighter. A pan crashes to the floor and the surfboard bumps against the side of the wall. He's never felt this before – this instability, this unsteadiness – not to this extent.

The van wobbles, rolls, and accelerates, as if skimming down the face of a wave, and then steadies and slows. With a gasp, she releases his head.

He climbs the curves of her body to her eyes, her wet and unforgettable eyes. He runs his hand over her smooth bald head and then below slides inside her.

He doesn't care about the Pacific Ocean swallowing the coasts or the fire melting the forests. He doesn't care that the air is fouled and the ocean increasingly un-swimmable. And he doesn't care about the injustice all around him, outside the walls of his van. He's not angry, not now. It's impossible to be angry now.

He's made mistakes, he'll admit that, and he's not so young either, can no longer pull off the surfer's arrogance and indifference he's cultivated. Not with her; she's too smart for that. He'll have to evolve is all, become something more than what he's been. And he'll have to come to terms with what he's done this day.

The van shimmies, slides forward. The lamp crashes. The Raphael falls. He realizes that they're floating away. The rising sea has lifted the van up and is pulling them out to sea in a rip. The sensation is instantly recognizable. He feels the familiar pull beneath the floor, the unconquerable current carrying them out to sea.

It's a massive surge and the van is heading out to sea. It must be a big quake, an epic swell with waves that could be surfed for a hundred miles. If he grabbed his board and paddled out the back door. His last session on the last seismic orgasm that was coastal California. That's legend. That's immortality. The only way to go.

But no, he'd rather be here with Bassia. Instead of whooping it up on the world's greatest swell, he'll stay here, in his old and dirty van, not riding on, but clinging to.

They're drifting away. She knows that now. The van is a boat; the floor a metal hull. Waves splash over the windows and onto the floor. It's impossible to tell which way is which.

They should get out.

They need to get out.

Urban's tongue is in her mouth, his hands are on her head and breast. She pulls him into her and feels a shudder, a rolling tremble. She can't tell if it's her body or the van. The mattress slides. A whirl of dust. A splash of cold. He groans.

She closes her eyes and settles back to bear the full force of the man and the ocean, the power and powerlessness. He's all over her now, in and out, mouth on mouth, chest on chest, legs intertwined, hands beneath. She pulls his ponytail and her remaining staccato thoughts – Sofina, injustice, the Goat, the governor, the departed artists, the cases on her desk – begin to shadow and fade. What does it matter who actually killed the former governor? Or why? Or who should be punished? Or why? Justice is as nebulous and preposterous as the people that pursue it.

She's on the mattress, alone with Urban, alone on the ocean and *this* too is enough. They will be miles out to sea. Until then, she will shudder, tremble, and roll.

She could become the lieutenant governor with a shot at governor when Sofina retires. It's tempting. Or she can renounce all of that and become something else, something new. She faces a choice as old as history: Diogenes or Alexander?

As Diogenes, she will not use logic and words, only counterbalance, illusion, and perspective: silent artistry. Quit the law and politics like a junkie going clean and live in Urban's van or one of her own. A hat for tips, a crate to stand on, a body to manipulate, a silent bow on the sidewalk – that is all.

Some will look at her and say, "Weren't you...?" and "Didn't you used to be...?"

As Alexander, she will take the oath of the lieutenant governor's office, swearing to defend the Constitution of the State of California against all enemies foreign and domestic. Embrace the tired words and abstractions, but perhaps, for once, with the power to make them work for her and others.

Some will look at her and say, "Did you ever perform...?" and "Didn't I once see you...?"

The van floats away, listing, rocking, and bobbing. Have they gone too far? Will they ever come back? Maybe the choice has been made. Maybe there is no choice.

She pulls him tighter.

47

Rex and Sofina have booked a presidential suite for the evening.

Their penthouse had been declared a crime scene, and there were too many people about, poking, clicking and ticking, dusting and vacuuming, sifting and repositioning. A cluster of forensic activity that they were "politely invited" to leave. They'd be "dutifully informed" when they could return.

They're on the top floor of the hotel because that's what wealth means: You're on top. Mountains, restaurants, hotels, other people; you're on top. As if the purpose of wealth is to unite the metaphorical and the literal. Rex chokes down a mouthful of bile and remorse and takes an inventory of his aches. His back and knees are starting to feel better along with the cut on his thumb, but the bruise on his tailbone makes it painful to bend over.

He stands with Sofina on the balcony and they stare at the shadowy outline of their city, ringed by an auburn tint of fire. He struggles with an increasing urge to confess. He should've remembered to take some antacid, though he's trying to stay away from all drugs at the moment, even the most benign. Who's to say an antacid would do any good? He's killed a man. Unintentionally, but there it is, as stark and irreversible as an amputation. He needs to tell someone – he's unnerved with compulsion – but the only someone he could tell is Sofina. Who just became governor but won't remain in that position if they discover that her husband assassinated the man who previously held it.

He'd made some bad decisions, a couple bad moves, and that's all it takes.

In his time as a teacher, he's known too many students who stepped into the wrong vehicle, turned at the wrong crosswalk, or swallowed the wrong substance. A misspoken word, a misplaced step, and they were assaulted or crippled, expelled or imprisoned. They'd lost lives, lovers, and friends within the folds of tragedy and parody, intention and consequence, the life we're given. The life we lead.

A groan in the walls, a grumbling behind them, and the balcony lurches forward and down. Sofina gasps and tries to figure the stability of the balcony, if it's constructed to code, if it's able to withstand the shuddering. A rumble from below and the street undulates like the flap of a towel. She feels the vibration though her feet. The scent of ash and burnt wood hits her moments later.

Should she make an announcement about the death of the governor? Should she inform her fellow citizens? No, there's enough going on to keep them occupied – is this the end of their great state? – and if they don't know who their governor is for a few more hours, no harm done.

The balcony bends perilously. She and Rex slip and regain their balance at a sharper angle. They grab the rail in front of them, then link their free arms and lean above the trembling city. The street has split open as if cleaved. Lights flash. A car on the far side sinks to its windshield, its alarm blaring. A flock of drones swoops down the street, transmitting the destruction from a safe altitude, lights blinking and cameras glowing.

If her mother could see her now, the most powerful person in the state and one of the richest. She was smart and worked hard, but she was lucky too. In so many ways. Her biggest stroke of luck was in having her mother and, perhaps, not a father. She's still an alien, looking down at her city, her state, and wondering what went wrong and how to fix it. Because humans have proven themselves to be worthless, cataclysmic.

She squeezes Rex's hand and recalls when he sauntered into her life with his blue eyes, self-effacing jokes, shifted Canadian vowels. Here he is now, quaking next to her, inhaling the same smoke, watching the same drones, with only themselves to blame and thank. The balcony jerks unevenly and in different directions. A fracture appears at their feet.

What's the rest of the country doing right now? What's happening in Boston, New Orleans and Salt Lake City? Beijing, Sao Paulo, Paris, and Dublin? California is the bellwether, the trendsetter, the forerunner, and what happens here will happen there soon enough. Soon they too will feel the squish in their shoes and taste the ash in their throats. They too will stand on failing balconies.

Rex feels Sofina's hand tighten around his as he watches the buildings of San Francisco sway like thick, metallic cornstalks. He swallows, sobering as the day's drugs recede, but with dread and guilt filling the vacancy. She turns her head to him, and he sees fierceness in her eyes. They hear screams from the room next door, sense the helplessness and vulnerability, but there is nothing he or anyone can do.

There is no sanctuary.

It no longer exists.

Surrender is the only option.

He must surrender to his addiction in order to defeat it. That's a beginning. And then perhaps, he can begin to support Sofina in her new job and see that his Eddie V and all his students get what they deserve. He needs to rediscover his purpose. Until then, he will continue to over-tip bad waiters, feed the homeless, recycle all he can, and try to wean his lust from powerful Nordic women. It's a start.

Now though, he will stand on the balcony with his wife, shuddering, breathing ash, and listening to the distant screams. No, he will not tell Sofina about what he has done. Not tonight. Or tomorrow. His crimes are his own. What he will do is confess it all in his poem. That'll have to suffice. That'll have to satisfy his urge to confess. He'll deliver one more ending in a story that already has too many. For there is always room for another ending, especially one that provides, for the few precious souls that will eventually read it, the true story of the former governor's death and his lovely wife's sudden rise to the state's highest office.

Sofina caresses Rex's fingers in hers. She won't tell him about the burden she's placed upon her sturdy shoulders, of seeding a new enlightenment, with extended rights and new definitions. Nor will she divulge to anyone her true ambition: that a reinvention of this state will be a reinvention of the country and, subsequently, a reinvention of the world. Her gifts have always been those of vision, scale, and scope. Share4All was never a niche player, and neither is she.

There will be skeptics as she is skeptical, but crises are opportunities and there have never been crises like these. The fires, the floods, an inhuman financial and technological economy, political paralysis, civil unrest, this quake, they have arrived simultaneously and synergistically.

The balcony sways forward and rebounds sharply. A weather drone crashes into the side of the building, collapses, and falls. For the first time, she understands that she may not make it. She's afraid but takes no account of her fear. Because her mission is unfinished. Because if there is a tomorrow, if the balcony holds and the sand bags hold, if the fire lines hold and the tectonic plates hold, then this night will be the harbinger of a new way. From the coastal swamps to the desert ashes, the survivors, if there are survivors, will re-create themselves and begin again.

For they are as she is.

They are as she is the desert cactus and the white-capped mountain. They are as she is the unbroken sky and grassy plain, as she is the fathomless ocean and swirling wind and scurrying creature. The teeming shore. There is nothing distinct, nothing separate, not anymore. Maybe there never was.

The building pitches and groans. Lights flicker and disappear. Glasses, tables, and chairs fall. A thunderous roar and the balcony becomes a springboard of cracks and concrete. A blue drone spirals to the ground and takes out two others. A large plume of ash explodes in the darkening sky.

The building falls forward, grinding and leaning toward the street at an unsustainable angle. She hugs Rex, and he hugs her back. Because they know that they're no longer safe. They need to scramble back into the building. Now. Before it's too late.

But no.

They will remain.

For they are as we are: farces and tragedies, eagles and scorpions, false and true prophets, sacred and desecrated, the burning, drowning, quaking hopes of the world.

The End

About the Author

David Hogan is a novelist, playwright and essayist. His debut novel, *The Last Island*, published by Betimes Books, was an Amazon Literary Bestseller in the U.K., reached No. 1 in Fiction at Amazon Australia and was a finalist for the San Diego Book Awards.

His stage plays include the New Play Initiative award-winning *Capital* and *No Sit – No Stand – No Lie*, which opened the Resilience of the Spirit Human Rights Festival in Southern California.

He is a contributor to *Writing.ie* and *IrishCentral.com* and a dual citizen of Ireland and the USA.

ALSO FROM BETIMES BOOKS

Dimitri Bortnikov
   Soul Catcher   ISBN 978-1-9161565-2-4

Fionnuala Brennan
   The Painter's Women:
   Goya in Light and Shade   ISBN 978-0-9929674-8-2

Hadley Colt
   Permanent Fatal Error   ISBN 978-0-9926552-6-6
   The Red-Handed League   ISBN 978-0-9934331-2-2

Les Edgerton
   The Death of Tarpons   ISBN 978-0-9934331-4-6

Sam Hawken
   La Frontera   ISBN 978-0-9926552-2-8

David Hogan
   The Last Island   ISBN 978-0-9926552-1-1

Kim Hood
   They All Fall Down   ISBN 978-1-9161565-1-7

Richard Kalich
  Central Park West Trilogy   ISBN 978-0-9926552-7-3
  The Assisted Living Facility
  Library   ISBN 978-0-9934331-9-1
  A Man Made Long Ago   ISBN 978-

Robert Kalich
  David Lazar   ISBN 978-1-9161565-0-0
  A Man Divided   ISBN 978-1-9161565-6-2

Patricia Ketola
  Dirty Pictures   ISBN 978-0-9934331-3-9

Jackie Mallon
  Silk for the Feed Dogs   ISBN 978-0-9926552-0-4

Donald Finnaeus Mayo
  Francesca   ISBN 978-0-9926552-3-5
  The Insider's Guide
  to Betrayal   ISBN 978-0-9934331-6-0

Craig McDonald
  One True Sentence   ISBN 978-0-9926552-8-0
  Forever's Just Pretend   ISBN 978-0-9926552-9-7
  Toros & Torsos   ISBN 978-0-9929674-0-6
  Roll the Credits   ISBN 978-0-9929674-1-3
  The Great Pretender   ISBN 978-0-9929674-2-0
  The Running Kind   ISBN 978-0-9929674-3-7
  Head Games   ISBN 978-0-9929674-5-1
  Print the Legend   ISBN 978-0-9929674-7-5
  Death in the Face   ISBN 978-0-9934331-0-8
  Three Chords & the Truth   ISBN 978-0-9934331-1-5

Borderland Noir (editor)   ISBN 978-0-9929674-9-9

Sean Moncrieff
    The Angel of the Streetlamps ISBN 978-0-9929674-6-8

Colin O'Sullivan
    Killarney Blues   ISBN 978-0-9926552-4-2
    The Starved Lover Sings ISBN 978-0-9934331-5-3
    The Dark Manual   ISBN 978-0-9934331-7-7
    My Perfect Cousin   ISBN 978-0-9934331-8-4
    Marshmallows   ISBN 978-1-9161565-4-8

Gérard Ramon
    In Love with Paris   ISBN 978-2-7466-8421-8

Kevin Stevens
    Reach the Shining River ISBN 978-0-9926552-5-9

Betimes Books is a non-profit literary publisher based in
Dublin, Ireland.

For more information please visit www.betimesbooks.com

ACKNOWLEDGMENTS

Many thanks to my first readers, Ismini Hogan and Jane Crooks, for their time, generosity, and insight.

Throughout the writing of this book, Jonathan Mack offered needed doses of friendship and advice.

I owe an ongoing debt of gratitude to the late, great Jerry Guardino, who remains a source of wisdom and inspiration.

I'm also grateful for the support and dedication of Svetlana Pironko, Maria Tirelli, and everyone at Betimes Books.

Lastly, thanks to my family for the love and the laughter.

www.ingramcontent.com/pod-product-compliance
Lightning Source LLC
Chambersburg PA
CBHW030656260626
47157CB00007B/2683